FACING JUSTICE

A Henry Christie Novel

Nick Oldham

This first world edition published 2011
in Great Britain and in the USA by
SEVERN HOUSE PUBLISHERS LTD of
9–15 High Street, Sutton, Surrey, England, SM1 1DF.
Trade paperback edition first published
in Great Britain and the USA 2012 by
SEVERN HOUSE PUBLISHERS LTD.

British Library Cataloguing in Publication Data

Oldham, Nick, 1956–
  Facing justice. – (A Detective Superintendent Henry
  Christie novel)
  1. Christie, Henry (Fictitious character) – Fiction.
  2. Police – England – Blackpool – Fiction. 3. Intelligence
  Officers – United States – Fiction. 4. Detective and
  mystery stories.
  I. Title II. Series
  823.9'2-dc22

ISBN-13: 978-0-7278-8075-8 (cased)
ISBN-13: 978-1-84751-374-8 (trade paper)

All Severn House titles are printed on acid-free paper.

Severn House Publishers support The Forest Stewardship Council [FSC],
the leading international forest certification organisation. All our titles that
are printed on Greenpeace-approved FSC-certified paper carry the FSC logo.

Typeset by Palimpsest Book Production Ltd.,
Falkirk, Stirlingshire, Scotland.
Printed and bound in Great Britain by
MPG Books Ltd., Bodmin, Cornwall.

To Belinda, my love

ONE

Massey was amazed to wake up alive. He was certain he'd be dead, that the horrific beating he'd endured – the fists, boots, sticks and bats – would have, *should have*, killed him. He'd obviously been lucid at the start of it, expecting to get a good hammering, basically what he deserved. But, only a short way into the assault, he realized this was much more than a punishment beating. He could tell by their faces and their eyes and their determination. And he knew this would be the last time he would ever be assaulted by anyone. But there had been nothing he could do about it. He couldn't protect himself or fight back in any way. Being securely gaffer-taped to a chair ensured that.

Then the pain took over, followed by the distortion of sight, sound and thought. Next the in-and-out of consciousness, vision blurring as though he'd opened his eyes deep under murky water, unable to see, then unable to feel, then unable to breathe. And then the merciful blackness of what he assumed was his death.

As consciousness returned, his eyelids fluttered but he didn't open them. Just lay there on the cold, gritty surface and explored how his body was feeling. He wasn't stupid enough to believe he would have fooled his captors into thinking he was still out of it. He knew he'd moved, knew he'd groaned, knew his breathing was in a different rhythm, but he didn't care. If they wanted to start on him again after they'd realized they hadn't killed him – which must have been their intention – eyes open or closed would not make one bit of difference.

Searing pain arced through his cranium, starting at a place just behind his eyeballs and radiating out in agonizing pulses, like a migraine times a thousand. Did this mean he had a fractured skull? He recalled the vicious stomp on the head that must have been the origin of the pain. That was when they'd got really carried away and lost it, after the chair had toppled over and one of them had jumped on him. His whole face had been forced out of kilter, distorted like a kid standing on a balloon.

Massey ground his teeth and moved the tip of his tongue along the back of them. Many were loose, hanging there in the gums, barely connected any more. There were two big gaps and he recalled spitting out fragments of crushed teeth when the men had heaved the chair back upright. He'd spat out the broken teeth and blood and squinted at the men through his pus-swollen eyes, then seen the baseball bat arcing towards him.

Now he did open his eyes. At least as far as they would open in the liquid-filled sacs of swellings now encasing them. He coughed, swallowed blood, and pain tore at his chest. Broken ribs? He moved a fraction, convulsing at the pain in his knees from the blows delivered by the bat.

He tried to control his breathing as a deep, long shudder passed like a ghostly shockwave through the entire length and breadth of his body.

He was in darkness, unable to work out where he was. So he lay still, moving his ankles and wrists slightly, realizing he was no longer taped to a chair, nor was there any duct tape binding his arms or ankles. He was lying on a hard floor now. He wondered if they thought they had succeeded in killing him, whether they had ripped the tape off and dragged him to this place that was like a basement of some sort. Somewhere to stash the body before disposing of it?

Massey brought up his legs, a movement that made him gasp. Then he eased himself very slowly and painfully up until he was sitting on his backside, still trying to control his breathing as if by doing so he could control the agony. He swayed a little, not wanting to move. What he wanted were painkillers and then to close his eyes and reawaken in a week's time, having healed.

Keeping his body as still as possible, he squinted at his location, and saw that he was definitely alone. They were not waiting for him to sit up just so they could begin again.

From what little light there was, it seemed as though he was in a basement room of some sort. A square room, not much bigger than a police cell – and he'd been in plenty of those in his time – with rough-hewn concrete flooring and inner walls constructed of breeze block. There was a tiny window, maybe a foot square, high up on one wall. Massey could see it was made from opaque, reinforced glass with three iron bars set into the window ledge.

And yes, he was definitely alone.

And there was a door.

Massey inched his head around and slowly tried to focus on it. It was steel-reinforced – another reminder of a cell, even down to the inspection hatch just below eye level. At ground level there was also a flap in the floor through which a food tray could be slid, something which puzzled Massey faintly. His eyes, though watery and swollen, were starting to work better now, seeing things more sharply even though he could not open them any wider than slits. The door had no handle on this side, so its locking was controlled from the outside. Again, just like a cell door, not a basement door.

He groaned involuntarily, spat something out that dribbled messily down his chin and on to his chest. He rocked, his head feeling as though lots of sharp stone chips were inside it.

But he was definitely alive. Of that he was certain.

Death, he now knew, had no feeling. Being alive meant sheer agony.

He wiped the back of his hand across his mouth. Then, closing one nostril with a finger, he blew down the open one, clearing it of blood and phlegm. He repeated the process with the other nostril.

His nasal passages clear, he smelled something other than his own blood and gagged at the odour. Something . . . a combination of heavy urine and dead flesh. Very strong and almost overpowering. A smell he could not place even though it was familiar and he had smelled it before. Sometime in his past, many years before. Or was it somewhere else in his memory, deep-rooted and primeval?

He shivered in fear.

'Fuck it,' he said and slowly curled his body around and eased himself up to his knees. He didn't stay in that position for long because his kneecaps had been hit by the baseball bat – but, as painful as they were, they had not been shattered. Then he recalled something else that puzzled him a little.

The man hitting his knees with the bat. And the other one holding him back. What had been said?

'No . . . don't break 'em. He needs to be able to . . .'

Massey tried to remember. Couldn't quite put the piece there.

'*Able to what?*'

'Fuck it,' he said again and pushed himself slowly up to his feet, then lost balance as everything inside his skull rolled loosely around. He staggered to the wall for support before he fell again, the palms of his hands holding him upright, his face just inches away from the breeze block.

He cursed and rested his forehead on the wall, then, puzzled, he drew back a few inches and made his eyes focus on a sign spray-painted on the wall. It was a diamond shape, basically an orange-coloured square tilted on to one of its corners. The word 'EXPLOSIVES' was written across it in thick black capitals. There was a graphic image above the word representing an actual explosion. Massey realized he was looking at a health and safety sign.

'What the . . .?' he started to say, thinking, *explosives in a basement?* But he could not be bothered continuing with the thought thread.

He inhaled another stuttering, painful breath, wincing as he felt the jagged end of a broken rib touching a lung. He turned, leaned on the wall, again exploring his current situation.

Despite the sign, the place did remind him of a basement, maybe situated under the main house. The ceiling seemed to be made of thick concrete and a light bulb dangled, unlit, on a foot-long thread of wire.

Then that smell. That odour. Where had he smelled it before? There was something horrible about it. Animal.

Using one hand on the wall for support he took an uncertain step towards the metallic door and stood in something soft. He looked down. It was shit. Despite his physical condition, Massey pulled a face and dragged his shoe across the floor to get it off his sole. He heard a click as the foot connected with and moved something.

This time it was a thick steel chain, one end sunk deeply and concreted into the wall. Massey reached for it and pulled it up. The links were heavy and strong. He ran them through his hands until he came to the end, attached to which was a leather collar two inches thick, one that would have fitted around the neck of the world's biggest dog.

Massey inspected the collar. It was made of thick but softly pliable leather with a big steel buckle. He held it to his bloodied nose and sniffed it cautiously. Then he dropped it as his guts spun over and he suddenly remembered where he had smelled that reek before – and realized that the stupid rumours he'd heard were true.

A very basic terror gripped him. Every hair on his body rose as adrenalin rushed into his system and drew blood away from the surface capillaries.

He moved quickly to the door. Fully expecting it to be locked, he ran his fingertips down the edge opposite the hinges and pulled at it. It creaked open an inch.

Massey paused. His senses tingled, heart pounded. He half expected them to burst in now, having realized their mistake in that they hadn't actually killed him. No one came. A cold, biting wind hissed through the gap, hitting his face with its iciness, and its freshness took away the odour of the room for a moment.

He opened the door a few more inches. Cautiously he peered out, still uncertain as to his whereabouts, but definitely not in the location in which he'd been assaulted. He edged out into a bright, moonlit, but excruciatingly cold night and seemed to be standing in the middle of nowhere. The world was completely silent, other than the sound of the wind. Not even distant traffic. And the room he had woken up in, thinking it had been a cellar under the main house, was nothing of the sort. It was the inside of a complete little building, about the size of a detached single garage. It was a sort of fortified hut, with one door, the high barred window and nothing else, with an outer perimeter twelve by twelve, maybe eight feet high and flat-roofed. The outer walls were thick stone. A sign on the door reiterated the inner warning: 'DANGER – EXPLOSIVES!'

His beaten, befuddled brain then realized where he'd been dragged to and dumped, and what the building was, or used to be.

He waited, listened for a few seconds, hearing nothing but the crash of his heartbeat. All he could feel now, even above the pain that wracked his injured body, was complete and utter fear.

He moved away from the building, limping, dragging himself along, knowing he had no time at all to worry about his wounds, what might be broken, damaged or bruised. Somehow he had to get away from this place. He forced himself to walk as quickly as he could across the barren, rocky ground, stumbling but managing to stay upright. He scrambled up an incline to the top of a mound of earth and stood squinting across a vast, open expanse in front of him, a huge black hole on the face of the world. But he did not pause for long. He moved on, hoping he had regained consciousness sooner than they thought he would.

He caught his foot, stumbled, fell, smacked down on to his sore knees, jarring his whole being. He cried out involuntarily and tried to muffle the noise, turning it from a scream of agony into a moan. But a noise nevertheless.

Then he was on his feet again, half sliding down a rubble-strewn slope and skidding into a wheel rut, cut deep into the clay.

Which way?

He started to follow the ruts, hoping there was some logic to this plan. Surely they would lead somewhere.

Once more he kicked a big stone and lurched. His body jarred and the broken rib touched his lung again, making him hiss with pain. He crumbled to the ground, waiting for the pain to ebb. Slowly it receded. He took a few more seconds for complete recovery.

Then, somewhere behind him, a slight scuffing sound. And another noise to accompany this: a rough, sawing cough.

The fear he felt intensified.

He rose slowly to his full height. Turned and looked into the darkness behind him. All his senses prickled. He was ready to flee.

Now he recalled what the man had said about his knees: 'Don't break 'em. He needs to be able to run.' Run! That was the word and Massey now knew why his knees hadn't been smashed and broken. It was always the intention that he would wake up. That he would live through the beating, as savage as it was. Intended that he had some ability to run, or at least hobble, on two feet. So he could take part in a dangerous race for his life.

He could not see or hear anything now. 'So it's true,' he said to himself. Then shouted, 'Come on you bastard,' into the dark.

And then he remembered that other thing. The stench. Now he placed it and he knew what was out there in the dark just beyond the periphery of his vision.

The moon had been covered by cloud which now peeled away and cast light across the rutted ground.

There were two short coughs.

Massey spun. He had been looking in the wrong direction. For a moment he was fixed to the spot, anchored by injury and terror, paralysed. Then he moved, but too late. His ankle twisted in a tyre rut, he screamed and went down. The last thing he saw were the two almond-shaped eyes reflecting silver in the moonlight.

TWO

Flynn immediately didn't like the guy. Smelled the stale alcohol on his breath, instinctively knew there would be trouble to come.

Had times been less harsh economically, Flynn would have told him the boat was fully booked and pointed him in the direction of one of the other charter fishing boats moored along the quay. But any charter is a good charter, Flynn's boss had told him, especially in this day and age. The fishing business had gone pretty limp over the last few months and there had been a rumour about mothballing some of the boats next month – January – if things didn't pick up. That meant no income from fishing and, for Flynn, a long, unpleasant spell as a doorman at one of his boss's clubs up in Puerto Rico's Commercial Centre.

So, quoting a vastly inflated price for the day that did not even cause the man to bat an eyelid, and separating him from 800 euros, Flynn said, please step aboard, sir. The only good side of it was that trailing behind the guy like a petulant teenager was his scantily clad lady friend, who looked as though she would rather be anywhere else in the world than climbing aboard a sportfishing boat in Gran Canaria. Her continually rolling eyeballs and accompanying body language told their own sorry story.

Flynn introduced the customer to Jose, his Spanish crewman, who extended his bear-paw of a hand to be shaken and was completely ignored by the man. Jose, undaunted, maintained his professional attitude and kept his broad grin in place as he withdrew his hand and redirected his attention to the even less receptive girlfriend.

She teetered up the gangplank on to the deck, losing one of her flip-flops into the water, and demanded, 'I want to be inside, I want food and booze . . . ugh, I feel sick already.'

'Your wish is my command,' Jose said and ushered her into the stateroom, passing within earshot of Flynn, mouthing a Spanish obscenity to him.

'Nah then, mate,' the customer said to Flynn, who hooked the floating flip-flop out of the water with a gaff, 'I'm told you're the best skip in the Canaries. Let's see, shall we?' He rubbed his hands and raised his face challengingly. 'If I don't come back having caught a blue marlin, I'll be really pissed off.'

'The marlin run ended late September,' Flynn told him. 'Won't be much chance of catching one, I'm afraid.'

'So what will we catch?'

'Maybe nothing, but there's plenty of thornbacks, stingrays and congers out there. Maybe lock into a shoal of tuna if we're lucky. Shark are always out there, too.'

'Don't want luck to be a part of it. You got fish finding equipment, haven't you? Sonar, y'know?'

'The most sophisticated and up to date,' Flynn confirmed. 'But even that doesn't guarantee fish.'

'Good job I know my stuff then, isn't it?'

'You're an experienced sport fisher?' Flynn asked as though he was interested.

'Oh yeah.'

Flynn waited, but there was no elaboration. 'I'll do my very best for you, then,' he assured the customer and began to prepare the boat – named *Faye 2* – for the day ahead.

The fishing turned out to be pretty good. No great monsters of the deep, but a fine array of specimens including a very meaty red snapper that Flynn kept and gutted, and would be his supper that night. The customer, whose name turned out to be Hugo, was kept reasonably happy and busy, though none of his claimed skills were either evident or tested much.

It was a different matter for his girlfriend, Janey. As the charter went on, she became progressively more seasick until she was begging Hugo to have the boat turned back to dry land. She had gone the colour of the decks, pure white, from an original golden brown tan, had spent some time with her head down the chemical toilet and even more hanging pathetically over the side of the boat, all sense of modesty having vanished as she hollered dreadfully at the sea gods.

Eventually she could bear it no longer. She dragged herself across the deck like a wounded animal to Hugo. He was strapped regally into the fighting chair with a rod rising majestically from his lower belly area. She begged him to end her misery.

Flynn watched the exchange from his lofty position in the flying bridge. It ended with Hugo roughly pushing Janey away. She fell flat on her backside and looked up appealingly at Flynn, as did Jose whose expression was a dark scowl of anger. Flynn sighed and slid down the ladder on to the deck. He helped Janey to her feet and back into the stateroom where she flopped on to the sofa and closed her eyes, gulping.

Then he spun back on to the deck and approached Hugo, who was still in the fighting chair.

'That's the end of the charter, sir,' Flynn told him.

Hugo's good-looking face turned towards him. 'Why would that be?'

'You want me to spell it out?'

'I think you'd better.'

'I don't tolerate your sort of behaviour on board.'

'What sort of behaviour is that?'

Flynn's chest tightened. He gestured to Jose. 'Bring in the rods, we're heading back.'

Jose nodded and grabbed one of the outriggers.

'I paid good money for this charter,' Hugo whined.

'You can have it back, less what it's cost so far.'

'Does that include this?' On his last word, Hugo pulled the rod butt out of the gimbal that was fixed to the leather pad worn around his waist and jettisoned the rod, reel and line out of his hands and into the churning sea behind the boat.

Flynn's mouth drooped in astonishment. Words began to form on his twisted lips, but before he could say anything, Hugo rose from the fighting chair, elbowed past him and stomped into the stateroom. Still not having said anything, Flynn watched him, utterly dumbfounded by his action.

Jose had witnessed the whole thing. He said, 'He threw that into the sea deliberately,' his Spanish tongue struggling slightly on the last word.

'I know,' Flynn said, turning desperately to the water to see if the rod was still there. It had disappeared instantly. Flynn's expression changed to anger and he took one step towards the entrance to the stateroom. Jose saw the alteration on Flynn's face – something he had seen too often recently, and invariably it meant trouble – and stepped in front of him, holding up one of his big hands.

'No boss, *nada stupido*.'

'I'm gonna launch that son of a—'

'NO,' Jose said firmly, looking into Flynn's eyes, holding his gaze.

Flynn ground his teeth, did a mental back-count from ten and took a deep breath. 'I'm OK.'

He went into the cockpit and grabbed the radio handset, pressed the transmit button, thinking he would call the coastguard and have them get the police to await their arrival back at port. Then he decided on a different approach. He ducked into the stateroom where a still sick Janey was laid out dramatically on the couch, eyes closed, a forearm covering her eyes. Hugo lounged in a chair, legs splayed, a bottle of San Miguel resting on his stomach. He glowered belligerently at Flynn.

'That gear's worth fifteen hundred euros.'

'And?' Hugo shrugged. 'Accident. Claim on the insurance.'

'Listen, bud, when we get back it can go one way or the other. First way, we go along to our quayside kiosk, you present your credit card and pay up. Second way – my preferred way – cops're waiting for you.'

'On what charge?'

'Criminal damage. Whatever way – no refund.'

'Do what you want.'

'Oh, just pay him,' Janey piped up from her sick bed. 'This whole holiday sucks.'

'Tell you what, Hugo, I'll have the cops waiting either way, eh?'

Hugo took a long, noisy draw from the bottle and scowled at Flynn. People seem to do that a lot, Flynn thought: glare at me.

'You're a big, hard man, aren't you, Mr Flynn?'

Flynn shook his head and sighed. He pivoted away, could not be bothered. 'Cops it is,' he murmured – but loud enough for Hugo to hear.

What he didn't expect was for Hugo to jump him.

Flynn patted Hugo's cheeks. 'C'mon, c'mon, wakey, wakey.'

Hugo had been placed in the recovery position – after Flynn had roared like a bear and thrown Hugo over his shoulder – and that was as long as the fight had lasted. Hugo smashed the back of his head on the corner of the door frame as he landed awkwardly and was knocked out instantly. Flynn had looked down at him in disbelief.

'The stupid . . .'

'Oh, what have you done?' Jose demanded, seeing the towering, muscled frame of Flynn standing over the unmoving body. Of a customer.

Flynn looked at him pointedly.

'He didn't do a thing,' Janey piped up despondently. 'Hugo went for him. He's like that, only he usually wins.' She propped herself up on one elbow, no colour whatsoever in her complexion.

Flynn gasped in exasperation and bent over to check Hugo's vital signs, which were fine. Even so, he hadn't recovered full consciousness by the time Flynn edged *Faye 2* back into her berth in the marina at Puerto Rico half an hour later. An ambulance was waiting on the quayside, as was Adam Castle, Flynn's boss and owner of the boat, as well as other boats and businesses. Castle slid the gangplank across to the stern and stood aside as two paramedics trotted aboard to tend to Hugo. Castle waited on the quayside, a stony, serious expression on his face.

Flynn briefed the medics and they carted a groggy, cross-eyed Hugo off into the ambulance.

Janey, having miraculously recovered from seasickness simply by standing on terra firma, made no attempt to join Hugo in the ambulance. She looked fine now.

'You not going with him?' Flynn asked.

'I don't think so. I'll catch up with him later.' She produced a wallet from the back pocket of her minute shorts. 'I'll pay for the fishing tackle. Hugo's credit card's in here and I know the PIN.'

'Thanks,' Flynn said.

The ambulance pulled away and Janey started to walk towards the booking kiosk, but paused, turned and looked meaningfully over her shoulder at Flynn. 'If you're interested . . . I'll be in the Irish bar in the Commercial Centre at eight tonight.'

'What about Hugo?'

'He won't be there, whatever.' She smiled. All her colour had returned and she was a completely different character to the one Flynn had been introduced to originally. 'Your choice, Flynn. One thing though – try not to bump into Hugo again. He bears grudges.'

He nodded graciously and then Adam Castle stepped into his line of sight. 'Words,' his boss said. 'Now.'

Castle led Flynn along the quayside, saying a great deal with just his body language. Flynn, big man that he was, followed meekly and they went all the way around the harbour into one of the first-floor cafés in the mini commercial centre overlooking the marina. Flynn sat glumly whilst Castle ordered a couple of Cruzcampos and set the chilled beers down on the table.

'Here, you're going to need this.'

Flynn was parched but he took the bottle cautiously and sipped the wonderful brew, rather than pouring it all down his throat in one, which was his instinct.

'Look boss,' he said, 'the guy went for me and I just reacted in self-defence. He'd been an arsehole all the charter; even his girlfriend was up to here with him.' Hell, his throat was dry and he spoke croakily, but necking the beer still seemed a little inappropriate to the circumstances. He was shocked by what Castle had to say next.

'I don't really give a monkey's about him, and I believe you, Steve – so as far as I'm concerned, there's no problem there.'

'Oh?' Flynn's eyebrows furrowed. 'So what's this about – the face and everything?' He wrapped his right hand around the bottle and lifted it to his cracked lips, deciding that a long slurp – not too long to be rude – was now OK. The ice-cold beer spread gratifyingly down into his chest.

Castle looked very troubled. He was chewing his bottom lip and shaking his head sadly.

'What is it, boss?' Flynn liked the guy. He had been very good to Flynn when he'd landed penniless on the island almost five years before. Had given Flynn a job on a boat, and Flynn had repaid him by becoming the best sportfishing skip on the islands. Flynn had grafted, learned his trade and applied his instinctual knowledge of hunting down the big fish, something that was innate and something most of the other charter skippers didn't have. Flynn also took out day safaris inland up into the mountains in the centre of the island and worked the doors of Castle's two night clubs when necessary. He had a lot to be grateful for to Castle.

'Don't know how to say this, pal . . . credit crunch and all that.'

Flynn ingested the words and his insides went even icier than the beer.

He went on, 'I'm a bit over-extended and I need to pull in the reins a bit, so I'll be mothballing the boats for two months because we haven't got one firm booking for that period and I can't rely on walk-ons.' He was referring to the ad-hoc customers who simply appeared at the boat, such as Hugo had done. 'Especially if you knock them all out,' he added lightly, but there was sadness in his voice. Castle had diverse business interests but particularly loved sportfishing. Flynn felt sorry for him.

'Every boat?' Flynn asked. There were half a dozen of them dotted around the Canaries.

'I won't lie to you – all but Orlando's in Tenerife. Business isn't quite as bad there, but everyone else will be out of the water.'

Flynn went hollow.

'I know you're ten times better than him, but Tenerife isn't suffering as much as Gran Canaria and you're here, not there. If it was the other way around . . .' Castle left the words unsaid. 'I'll review the position at the end of January.'

'So I'm out of a job?'

'For the time being. If you want to try and find work with any of the other charters, I'll understand.'

Flynn scrunched up his face. 'What about Jose? He has a wife and kid to look after.'

Castle shrugged. Not as if to say 'Whatever,' but as though the whole thing was tearing him apart. 'I'm closing down two of the bars, too. It's like a ghost town on the Centre, but I'll keep the Irish-themed bar ticking over. You can do the door there, if you like. And if I get any bookings for the jeep safaris you can take them out. I'm keeping the travel agency open.'

Flynn inhaled deeply and rubbed the back of his neck. 'You going to tell Jose?'

Castle nodded, finished his beer and rose from the table. Flynn watched him wend his way back to the quayside, shoulders slumped, then head towards *Faye 2*. Flynn ordered another beer, this time in a glass, and sipped it slowly, his mind working the angles. So for at least the best part of two months he would be ashore and effectively out of work. Chances were the Irish wouldn't open every day of the week and the money from doing the door would be spasmodic at best.

He mulled over the possibility of approaching another charter boat but could not convince himself it was a good idea. They were all struggling with a shortage of demand. Even the annual regulars weren't re-booking. And he'd feel uncomfortable on another boat. He had a history with *Faye 2*. She had been his choice of vessel when the original *Lady Faye* went up in a ball of flame and exploding gas bottles. He had worked with the replacement and knew her intimately, her foibles, her strengths, her weaknesses. And he worked well with the Spanish curmudgeon that was Jose, even though their relationship was often fraught. So even if he could, he probably wouldn't go to another boat.

The ice in the beer glass rose languidly to the surface. Flynn watched it as he also mulled over the financial aspects of the situation. He had very little money stashed, had recently moved to a small apartment which required him to fork out a nominal rent. Probably had about four months before he needed to start looking seriously for work, six before times would become desperate.

He uttered a short internal laugh and took a long draught of the beer. In spite of the circumstances he felt in reasonable spirits. Things weren't half as bad as they had been five years earlier when he'd been effectively drummed out of the cops with a very black rain cloud hovering over his head, been thrown out by his wife who afterwards had shacked up with his best friend and prevented him from making any contact with their son Craig, then ten years old. Those had been bleak times and he had come through them, more or less, even if his past had managed to creep up on him in a most unpleasant way about a year ago.

Flynn wondered if the bleached bones of the two men would ever be discovered in that inaccessible gully near the Roque Nublo up in the mountains. He doubted it. He smiled grimly at the memory, then shrugged it off and thought that something would turn up.

He fished his mobile phone out of his pocket, switched it on and waited for it to find a signal. It bleeped, telling him he had received a voice message whilst the phone had been switched off. There was no number or name recorded but it did state it had come from an international number.

Flynn grinned with pleasure. He expected it would be a message from Craig. Following the events of the previous year, contact between the two had been re-established with the consent of Flynn's ex-wife. Craig had even been allowed to come out to the island for two weeks over the summer holiday when they'd worked together on the boat. It had been a wonderful fortnight and he'd re-bonded with Craig. When the lad had returned to the UK, both had been heartbroken.

He dialled the answerphone service and waited for the connection, fully expecting to hear Craig's still childlike voice.

But the voice he heard was not that of his son.

It was a thin, desperate-sounding female voice, one that Flynn recognized immediately.

'Flynnie? Flynnie? It's me . . . Cathy . . . hi, hope you're OK, big guy.' Flynn heard what he thought was a sob. 'Sorry, sorry . . . look, Flynnie, can you give me a call? I'm . . . I don't know what to do or who to turn to . . . God, it sounds so pathetic, but' – another sob – 'it's just going all wrong, everything, please . . . gimme a bell . . . I know you're two thousand miles away . . . need someone to talk to, to talk it out . . .'

The robotic voice of the answerphone lady came on. 'End of messages. To play this message again, press one . . .'

Flynn pressed one and listened hard to the message again. The phone then beeped and the screen display told him another voice message had landed from the ether. He listened to the new one.

This time the voice was even more fraught. 'Flynnie, it's me again, Cathy, you're probably getting sick of hearing me by now. God, this must be the eighth time of trying . . . need to see you, talk to you, mate . . . please, please call me.'

The message ended but before Flynn could do anything more, four more landed in quick succession.

THREE

Preston Crown Court. Court Number One. Shell-shocked and evidence weary, the jury of eight men and four women shuffled back into the court room for the last time, having reached their verdict after four days of heated deliberation. They sat meekly, avoiding eye contact with the accused.

Detective Superintendent Henry Christie noted the body language and as usual, when he became excited at the possibility of a result, his bottom clenched tightly. He exchanged a very quick glance with the detective inspector sitting next to him, Rik Dean. A glance of triumph. Both men could smell it. Surely this had to be a guilty verdict.

The investigation had been long and difficult, understaffed and fairly low-key, even though the police were hunting a professional killer who had executed a gangland lord by the name of Felix Deakin. Having escaped from custody, Deakin himself had been on the run from the police; tracked by the cops to an isolated rural farmhouse, he had been re-taken into police custody but before the police had even managed to put him in the back of a van, the hit man had struck. From his hiding place up on the moors, almost a mile away, he had expertly blown Deakin's head apart with a high-powered rifle. He had escaped before the stunned police could react.

Henry was convinced the killer had been hired by one of Deakin's rivals, a man called Jonny Cain, because Deakin had volunteered to give crucial evidence against Cain in a murder trial. Although Henry was certain of this, certainty didn't mean evidence, but it was a starting point for what was only part of a complex investigation with many threads.

Setting a small team to work consisting of experienced detectives, intelligence and financial analysts and firearms officers, Henry let them get on with the job. Five months down the line they had a name. From the name came various aliases. From the aliases, bank accounts across the world, complex travel arrangements, forensic tie-ins – and then the location of the individual.

Working with Interpol and the Cypriot police, an armed raid was carried out on a secluded villa near Paphos and a man arrested without any bloodshed or drama.

Three months later, after much solid detective work assisted by a forensic team that managed to link the man in custody to the position he'd laid up in with his rifle (not recovered) on the bleak moors of Rossendale, he was in crown court facing a murder charge, even though he had not said one word whilst in custody. But that didn't matter.

And now the jury was back.

Henry held his breath as the clerk of the court asked the jury foreman if they had reached their verdict.

The man stood nervously, as though his back was killing him. His eyes did not look into the steel-grey impassive eyes of the killer in the dock. He said, 'Yes we have, Your Honour,' addressing his reply to the judge.

Henry glanced at the defendant. He was ex-army, had been a sniper in Kuwait, Iraq and Afghanistan – a superb one – and had left the services and offered his killing skills to the highest bidder. He had an exemplary service record and no previous convictions, facts referred to many times by the smooth defence barrister. But Henry knew he had carried out at least four other assassinations in African republics that had netted him about a million and a half pounds, probably foreign aid money. The killing of Felix Deakin had brought him two hundred thousand, money that was still being tracked by the financial experts, but it was proving tricky to find the source.

The man, who was called Mike Calcutt, allowed his gaze to take in the jury foreman and Henry – pausing just a little too long for comfort on the detective – before looking back at the jury.

The clerk asked if the verdict reached was unanimous or by a majority.

'Unanimous.'

A whisper of amazement flitted around the public galleries, which were packed with gawping public and greedy media.

The clerk then read out the murder charge against Calcutt and asked if the jury found him guilty or not guilty.

For a brief moment, as the foreman paused, Henry thought he was witnessing some reality TV show, where contestants were voted off.

'Guilty.'

Henry's eyes swept to Calcutt. He did not flinch. Cool, cool bastard, he thought. But we got you in the end. If only we could get the bastard who hired you in the first place.

Henry, Rik Dean and four other detectives involved in the case had gathered in a loose congratulatory circle in the public waiting area outside the court-room doors. They all beamed wide smiles and there were lots of handshakes and high-fives amongst them. The kind of euphoria that comes after a protracted, successful investigation that nails a killer.

'Well done everyone,' Henry said, checking his watch. He meant what he said, because he'd very much taken a back seat and had only put his twopenn'orth into the machine when asked. Now that he was a detective superintendent he was trying to delegate more and not get involved in day-to-day investigating. It went against his natural instinct, as was the case with most high-ranking detectives who loved to get down and dirty with the lads. Problem was that it was easy to lose sight of the overview and at his rank, as he was learning, that was not something he could afford to do. He had now become a professional plate spinner and this major inquiry was just one of many he had to manage.

'Drinks?' Rik Dean suggested. There was an eager gaggle of yeses from his colleagues, who wanted to celebrate in the traditional way.

This was although the defendant had yet to be sentenced by the judge. Once the jury had informed the court of the verdict, the defence had immediately leapt up with a desire to make submissions, so the judge had adjourned proceedings when he would hear further bleating from Calcutt's defence. Then he would sentence him to life imprisonment, the only available option in the case of murder.

'You guys go ahead.' Henry delved into his jacket, extracted his wallet and pulled out fifty pounds, which he gave to one of the jacks. 'Have a round on me. I need to—' He was interrupted by the arrival of a court usher.

'Detective Superintendent Christie?'

'That's me.'

'Message from the holding cells . . . Mr Calcutt wishes to speak to the senior investigating officer before he's taken on remand.'

Henry looked blankly at the black-smocked man. 'You mean the defendant, Calcutt?' The other detectives had become silent.

'Yes sir, his brief asked me to pass on the message.'

Henry squinted, then looked at Rik Dean. 'You're the man,' he said. 'Take one of the other guys with you. Your job, I'll leave it with you.'

Henry strode out of the court and stood on the mezzanine. It had become brutally cold outside and he shivered as he slid himself into his Crombie. His first impulse had been to grab Rik and head down to the cells and see what was behind this turn-up for the books. But he would have been butting in. It was effectively Rik's investigation and Henry was happy to leave it to him. He had been angling to get Rik on to the Force Major Investigation Team (FMIT), which he jointly headed, and it had taken some persuading to get the nod for Rik to run this investigation. Now that it had proved to be successful, Henry hoped he would be able to convince the chief constable that Rik should have a permanent position on the team. If something came out of speaking to Calcutt, then all the better.

He pulled out his mobile phone, switched it on, called home. 'Has Karl landed yet?' he asked Kate, his wife.

'Just this minute pulled up outside.'

'Great. Hey – see you soon. And we got a result here, by the way.'

'Ooh, you are such a good detective,' Kate cooed mockingly. Henry didn't pick up on the lack of sincerity and said, 'I am, aren't I?' without a trace of irony.

Flynn took the decision to avoid the Irish bar when he turned out late that afternoon, suspecting that an encounter with Janey might lead to complications he could well do to avoid. After showering and dressing in the tiny terraced villa he rented, he wandered back down to the harbour and trotted down the steps into one of the bars in the complex at the back of the beach itself, wearing his beloved Keith Richards T-shirt and three-quarter length pants. It was still early and quiet, but Flynn knew it was unlikely to get any busier. Many bars were struggling to survive in the economic downturn as tourists kept their own heads down and shied away from foreign holidays. This was one of Flynn's regular haunts and had managed to keep going by providing bargain booze and inexpensive but good food. The manager smiled at Flynn's arrival and immediately filled a half-litre glass with Estrella Damm, placing it in front of Flynn, together with a small plate of olives, as he nestled up to the bar. Flynn nodded and sipped the ice-cold beer.

'You eating, Señor?'

Flynn had intended cooking the red snapper caught earlier by Hugo, but couldn't be bothered. It was in the fridge, would keep until the day after.

'I think so, Manny.'

A menu appeared in front of him as if by magic. Flynn chose paella for one, which he knew would take about twenty minutes to prepare. He slid off the bar stool and said, 'I'll eat outside.' He took his beer and olives and walked to one of the tables on the decking erected over the sand.

It was still warm, twenty-eight degrees, and Flynn settled into one of the big, comfy chairs and soaked in the heat. He loved it. He had been out on the island for almost five years now and the pace of life, the people and the lifestyle had really taken a grip of him.

He took out his phone and tried, not for the first time, to return the call from Cathy James.

He waited patiently for the connection, but when it went through, the answering service cut in. His mouth warped with frustration. He placed the phone on the table, pulled his baseball cap down over his eyes and reached for the beer, wondering what the hell she could want.

She had sounded troubled and unhappy. Totally different to the last time Flynn had seen her.

That had been in October last year when she and her new husband, Tom James, had come out to the island for their honeymoon. Flynn had been unable to get to the UK for the wedding, so he had tried to make amends by finding a villa for them – for free – and picking them up from the airport. He had also arranged a fishing trip and a jeep safari, both at no cost, and they seemed to have had a great time.

Flynn and Cathy went way back. He had met her when he joined Lancashire Constabulary after leaving the Marines over twenty years ago. They had been new recruits at the same intake, he being a bit older than her at twenty-three, she nineteen, shiny, straight out of the box, a bit naive, but extremely beautiful.

At the time she had been single and he'd been married. This hadn't stopped them from becoming lovers for a very brief time, though ultimately they became just very good friends. As their careers moved off in separate directions, they kept in contact but hardly saw anything of each other in the years that followed. Flynn knew she got married and then divorced, while he had remained spliced until both his job and relationship went south and he ended up quitting the cops and taking up residence in Gran Canaria.

It was during the period he was under investigation that he re-established contact with Cathy. By then she was seriously into a relationship with a detective from Lancaster, who she married a few years later – hence the provision of a honeymoon by Flynn.

Flynn raised his eyes and looked across the beach, watching holiday-makers trudge through the gentle surf at the water's edge.

He wondered if something had gone wrong with the marriage, Cathy's second. Was that why she was calling him, wanting to talk? He hoped it was something much less complicated, but couldn't guess what. He wasn't a good counsellor, but a man of action who wasn't anywhere near in touch with his feminine, touchy-feely listening side.

Cathy and Tom had seemed a perfect couple, but wasn't that what honeymoon couples usually appeared to be? Flynn remembered discreetly watching her on the day he took them out fishing. She had been all goo-goo eyes for Tom, the new hubby. Couldn't stop watching him, hanging on his every word. Flynn had actually felt some mixed emotions at that point.

First and foremost he was happy for Cathy. She had been through a bad time, had had a terrible first marriage, really been through the mangle. Then she'd found Tom, who on the face of it came across as a caring, generous guy, and she was head over heels in love with him. On the flip side, Flynn had felt a pang of envy. Not many months before he thought he had been on the verge of finding the love of his life, but had lost her tragically. The third side of the coin, if there was such a thing, was that Flynn also thought about what *could* have been with him and Cathy, had the timing been right. They had probably been in love, he thought, way back when – whatever love meant, he thought cynically. Maybe things would have been very different if both had been free to pursue their relationship beyond a fling at a police training centre. Instead, they had accepted that their only future was as mates.

Cathy – maybe, it seemed – had also harboured the same wistful idea. She had caught Flynn looking at her and sidled up to him, out of sight and earshot of Tom. She was down to a skimpy bikini and her body was still slim, yet plump in all the right places – just as Flynn remembered it all those years before. She gave him a loving hug and whispered into his ear, 'Oh, what could have been.'

'I reckon you've got a good man,' Flynn said, trying to hide the rush of blood her proximity had given him.

'Yeah, I have. He's a good man, you're right.' She glanced over at Tom who was harnessed in the fighting chair, being attended to by Jose. Then her face turned to Flynn. 'Thanks for this,' she said.

'It's what friends are for.'

'I just wish you were as happy.'

Flynn chortled. 'One day I will be.'

'Good. I hope so, Flynnie.' She touched his face gently with her fingertips. 'Always be there for you, y'know, y' big lug.'

'And me for you,' he promised.

But then that little moment of tenderness was shattered by Jose's booming Spanish-accented voice. 'Big one, boss!'

Flynn looked up. Two hundred metres off the stern of the boat was almost certainly the biggest, and the last, blue marlin of the season, rolling magnificently through the waves. Flynn jumped into action and with his skill as the best skipper in the Canaries – something he rarely let Jose forget – took the bait to the fish and brought in a seven hundred pounder that had the newly married Tom fighting a battle that lasted almost two hours.

Halfway though the contest, Flynn had said to Cathy, 'I hope you weren't planning any conjugals tonight. After this I don't think he'll be able to lift a pint, let alone . . . you know.'

'In that case he'll have to lie there and take it – just like you used to do.' Cathy laughed lustily and screamed with glee as the magnificent fish leapt a dozen feet out of the blue sea in an effort to shake loose the steel hook. Its muscular body writhed and twisted before it fell back into the water and dived deep into the ocean.

Flynn blinked himself back to the present day as his seafood paella arrived, decorated with pink langoustines, still in the shell. Flynn took one, burning his fingers, cracked open the hinged body to access the lovely white flesh within. With the assistance of another beer, he wolfed down the dish, then sat back to let it settle.

It was slightly cooler now, a breeze getting up, but still plenty warm to sit out, something rare in the UK, he thought, even in summer.

His mobile rang.

'Steve Flynn.'

'Flynnie . . . Flynnie . . . oh, thank God I got you.'

'Cathy? What the heck's going on? I tried to call you back loads of times. Are you all right, love?'

He heard her choke. 'No, no, not really.'

'What's up then?'

'Steve, can you come back? I know it's a big ask . . . but I need to talk to you. I need a friend I can trust.'

'Cathy, what is it?'

'Look, I can't talk over the phone. Steve, it's Tom.'

'Is he OK?'

'Flynnie, I don't know who to turn to.'

'Cathy, what's happening?' he asked firmly.

'I think . . . I know . . . oh, God . . .'

'What do you know?'

'Flynnie, I think Tom's on the take.' She paused. 'I mean big style. He's a bent cop.'

FOUR

It was one of those slightly potty middle-aged-man ideas that usually don't get anywhere. A product of a conversation loosened by alcohol which no one took seriously at the time but which planted a seed and was remembered.

The main problems were of logistics, workload and opportunity.

Both men were horrendously busy.

Henry Christie, as joint head of FMIT, had many serious enquiries to oversee, committees and working parties to attend nationally and locally. All that in itself would have been fine if the world stood still, but it didn't, it continued to revolve relentlessly. People did not stop murdering others; long-running investigations didn't suddenly get cleared up and there was always some new initiative that needed the presence of someone at Henry's rank to make it happen.

Karl Donaldson, Henry's American friend, worked as an FBI legal attaché at the US embassy in London. He, too, was over-whelmed with work. Fundamentally he was an analyst and liaison officer, making and forging links between law enforcement agencies across Europe, from the UK to Russia. At the same time he often made forays into the field, sometimes finding himself in dangerous situations, whether coming face to face with a wanted terrorist or dealing with corrupt factions in his own organization.

The two men had first met over a dozen years before. Their paths had crossed when Donaldson, then a full-time FBI field agent, was investigating American mob activity in the north-west of England. Henry, then a detective sergeant, had encountered the Yank when an investigation he was pursuing became explosively intertwined with Donaldson's. They had made friends hesitantly at first, but as their personal and professional lives continued to criss-cross over the years, they became good pals.

It also helped that Donaldson had met, fallen in love with and subsequently married a Lancashire policewoman. Even though she had subsequently transferred to the Metropolitan Police to be near Donaldson's work in London, her northern connections often brought the both of them up past Watford regularly. His wife, Karen, also became good friends with Henry's on-off-and-on wife, Kate.

A couple of months earlier, Donaldson had been in Lancashire on business – something hush-hush he could not even begin to reveal to Henry – and when it was completed he had stayed on at Henry's for a couple of nights. On one of those nights, they had hit Henry's local, the recently refurbished Tram & Tower.

They'd reminisced over a few pints, Donaldson becoming increas-ingly garrulous after his intake: he was a big man, six-four, as broad as a bear, but he couldn't hold his drink. Anything over two pints and he started to lose control. Henry, on the other hand, raised in the seventies and eighties culture of the cops, always remained steady, although he didn't actually drink much these days as he grew older.

'Y'know, man,' Donaldson slur-drawled in his soft American accent, 'I love ya, man.'

They were seated in one of the newly constructed alcoves of the pub, chatting and paying passing attention to the newly introduced 'Kwiz Nite' hosted by the landlord, Ken Clayson.

Henry squinted at Donaldson's revelation.

'No, I mean, you're a guy who's always on the edge, but I kinda like that.'

'Right.' Henry drew out the word.

'Hey! You thought about having any more kids?'

Now Henry screwed up his face. 'That's a resounding no.'

'God, I can't wait,' Donaldson said, misty-eyed. He had – accidentally – made Karen pregnant but now he couldn't wait to be a father again, even though they already had two kids who were just into their teens.

'I'm too old, and so is Kate,' Henry said. 'We've only just got rid of the two daughters as it is – and they keep bouncing back like they're on elastic bands. It's chill time, pal.'

'Karen's no spring chicken,' Donaldson pointed out.

'How gentlemanly,' Henry remarked. 'Is everything going OK?'

'Aw, hell yeah. Child-bearing hips, y'know. She's blooming – and the pregnant sex is awesome.'

'Whoa.' Henry made the number one stop sign. 'Too much. Anyway, glad to hear things are fine, but it'll put the brakes on everything else,' he warned his companion.

Donaldson sipped his third lager ruminatively. 'Guess so.' His voice was wistful. Then, 'Hey! I have an idea.'

'Go on.'

'Before she gives birth, how about you and me sneaking away for a night or two of debauchery? Wet the baby's head before it arrives.'

'If I recall, the last time you were off the leash, you debauched a little too much.'

Donaldson looked sheepishly at Henry, his mind full of the one and only time he had been unfaithful to Karen. In a hotel room in Malta with a Scandinavian lady who had subsequently bombarded and terrified him with obscene e-mails with photographic attachments. 'I was thinkin' more of a guy thing. Not sure what, though.'

'Whatever, it would have to be short and sweet, I guess. How about a walk and an overnighter?'

'A walk? Do you walk?'

'I've been known to put one foot in front of the other occasionally. We could set off over the hills one day, overnight in a village pub somewhere, then walk on. Park a car at either end, something like that.'

Donaldson thought about it. 'Lake District, you mean?'

'Possibly,' Henry shrugged.

'And now for round two of our Krazee Kwiz Nite.' Their conversation was interrupted as the voice of Ken, the landlord, boomed out over the PA system. 'Pens and answer sheets at the ready. Next ten questions are on the hits of the sixties.'

'Ahh,' Donaldson said, 'your era.'

'You ain't far behind, pal.'

There was no more talk that night of a boys' break, but it was a thought that remained with them, nagging away at the back of their minds.

Jack Vincent sat in the battered chair at the battered desk inside the stolen mobile cabin that doubled as his office and a refreshment area for the workers in the quarry that deeply scarred the hillside a quarter of a mile away. Vincent's cruel face set hard as he shivered and hunched himself deeper into his thick donkey jacket. The gas heater was on, but fighting a losing battle against the harsh north-easterly wind that swooped down from the moors above the village of Kendleton in north Lancashire. Keeping any warmth in the cabin was a constant battle as the outside temperatures continued to tumble with the approach of evening.

From Vincent's position, looking out from the cabin, he could monitor any traffic approaching the quarry up the steep winding lane from the main road. He could watch his heavy lorries as they reached another cabin where they booked in and then were sent on the right-hand fork through the gates into a steel-walled compound. Here any 'necessary changes' were attended to by Vincent's fitter, before they were sent on towards the loading area, where the crushing and filtering machines smashed the rock that had been blown out of the quarry face, then graded it to customer requirements. The lorries were then refilled and sent back out on the road.

At the moment, Vincent's main customer was a huge multinational road-building company subcontracted by the Department of Transport to widen a stretch of the M6 near Stafford. It was a government contract worth several million pounds and Vincent had manoeuvred brutally to get his piece of it. There had been the necessary payoffs, a bit of very heavy intimidation against his rivals – because a well-paid contract like this was always hard fought for by the minnows – and one particularly nasty incident where Vincent and his silent partner had been forced to resort to whacking the edge of a shovel into a man's head. There was now nothing left of that man. He had been fed limb by limb into a crusher, mixed in with a few tons of hardcore, and was buried underneath a bridge pillar on the stretch of motorway he had, ironically, been so keen to build.

Vincent checked his watch, a Rolex, incongruous against the sleeve of his grubby donkey jacket, then peered down the twisting track.

Two empty lorries were expected. Their fourth run of the day. And, like clockwork, they appeared. They were huge monsters, but even they were overshadowed by the giant machines that worked the quarry itself.

Vincent smiled and his face softened with triumph. There would be something extra for each of these vehicles when they left the quarry with the many tons of ground rock in them. He stood up.

The first of the lorries drew up at the reception cabin. The driver dropped out of the cab. He went in and did some paperwork with the woman who dealt with admin, the dispatch and return of orders. Then he clambered back and drove through to the compound, pulling up with a hiss of airbrakes under a drive-through awning constructed of corrugated metal. He got out of the cab again and turned to Vincent, who had walked in behind.

'The Department of Transport and the cops have set up a couple of stop-checks on north and southbound at Charnock services on the M6,' he told Vincent.

'Make sure you don't stop there for a brew, then,' Vincent replied to the driver, who was called Larry Callard.

'Just saying – they're out and about and me and Bert have already exceeded our hours today. If we get pulled, we're screwed.'

As they were talking, a man clad in overalls, rubbing his hands with an oily cloth, strolled across to them. He was big and broad, early forties, with deep-set eyes and a ruddy complexion. This was 'Ox' Henderson, Jack Vincent's vehicle fitter.

'What's up, boss?'

'Department's out and about.'

'And my hours are way over,' Callard whined.

'Can you fix it?' Vincent asked Henderson.

'Fix anything.' He heaved himself into the cab of Callard's lorry, lay across the seat and reached down to the tachograph, the device fitted underneath the dashboard that recorded drivers' hours on a plastic-coated disc. It was supposed to be tamper-proof. Many people, however, had found ways and Henderson was a bit of an expert with them. He had once been the transport manager of a small, criminally run haulage business, but when the company had been investigated by the ministry and the police, Henderson's way with a tachograph had been uncovered. He had been hung out to dry by the company owners, found himself behind bars for fraud for three months and then completely unemployable. Until Jack Vincent took him on.

'Go grab a brew,' Henderson shouted from the cab. 'Be about ten minutes here, then no one'll even know you've ever been out on the road today.' He laughed.

Callard turned to leave. Jack Vincent's spidery hand grasped his arm. 'You having problems, Larry? I'm picking up a vibe, mate.'

'What do you mean?' He looked nervously at Vincent.

'I mean you do what I say and you get paid well for it – yeah? I don't want no moaning, otherwise . . .'

'I wasn't moaning.'

Vincent held Callard's eyes meaningfully for a long second. Then he nodded as an understanding passed between them.

'There'll be something extra in the next run. I'll give you details on the way out, OK? Usual bonus.'

'Yuh, whatever, boss.'

Vincent's fingers uncurled from Callard's forearm and he nodded curtly. The second of the returning, empty lorries pulled into the awning. As the driver climbed out, Vincent said to him, 'See Ox.' He jerked his thumb in the direction of the first lorry, and Henderson's booted feet sticking out of the cab as he worked on the tachograph. 'Then grab yourself a brew – but I want you back on the road in half an hour.'

'No probs, boss,' the second driver said. His name was Bert Pinner.

Yeah, Vincent thought as he walked back towards the cabin, his head tilted against the biting wind, never is a problem with you, Bert. But I'm starting to get mighty concerned about Callard.

Whatever, this would be the last run of the day for the two lorries. By the time they'd had their tachographs fixed, then reloaded with hardcore and been sent on their way, done the delivery down the M6 – plus the extra side-bits – it would be almost ten at night.

No other traffic was due to be coming up to the quarry, so Vincent jarred to a halt when he saw a pair of headlights bouncing up the track. He stood by the door of the cabin, collar pulled up, and waited for the vehicle to arrive, which it did a few moments later, skidding to a grit-crunching stop on the stony ground.

It was a big four-wheel drive Land Cruiser, with greyed-out windows, similar to the kind of thing Vincent drove whilst on quarry business. Difference was this one was newer, cleaner and a better model. The doors opened and two men got out.

And Jack Vincent cursed himself. He wondered how quickly he could get into the cabin and reach the sawn-off shotgun he kept Velcroed under the desk, always fully loaded, usually within hand's reach.

Instead, he affixed a tight smile and approached the men, hand outstretched, the very model of welcome.

Henry and Donaldson decided to try the new menu at the Tram & Tower, which was mostly based around chicken: roast chicken, fried chicken, piri-piri chicken – and chips with either peas, carrots or salad. It was not terribly inspired and when this was delicately pointed out to the proud landlord, Ken, he looked crestfallen and pouted from underneath his beard.

'All the products are sourced locally,' he defended his menu at the newly created 'Food Ordering Point' at one end of the shiny new bar. He glared at Henry and Donaldson, daring them to challenge his statement. They hid their eyes behind the huge laminated menus and exchanged a look of fear. They did not want to upset a tame landlord. 'And,' Ken declared, 'I've got new chef. He's brill.'

'OK, OK,' Henry said to pacify him. 'I'm sure it'll be great. I'll have the piri-piri and Karl will have the roast breast wrapped in bacon . . . both with chips, obviously.'

Clayson entered the order into the new till with a flourish, then extended his hand for payment. 'Twenty-seven pounds and fifty pence.'

'Sheesh,' Henry muttered. 'It's not cut price then?'

'You can't cut corners with quality. And that does include your drinks and a free trip – once only, mind – to the salad bar.'

Henry inserted his debit card into the machine and tapped in his PIN. Clayson tore off the receipt and handed it over, together with a wooden spoon with a number painted on it.

'What's this for?' Henry asked. 'Don't we get cutlery any more?'

Clayson gave him an expressionless stare. 'Stick it in the empty wine bottle on your table and the waitress will find you. Enjoy your meals,' he added smarmily.

The two men turned away from the bar with their drinks and found a table in an alcove. After clearing a space amongst the salt, pepper and cutlery containers that seemed to take up most of the table, Henry laid out an Ordnance Survey map, easing out the folds. Then he raised his pint of Stella Artois and clinked glasses with Donaldson, who was drinking the same.

'To a bit of a lads' adventure, eh?'

Vincent knew one of the men, but not the other. The Land Cruiser's driver was the one he hadn't come across before and he could tell, pretty much, that he'd simply come along to help provide some intimidatory support for the passenger.

Not that he needed any help. Because the rangy black guy, who was called H. Diller, had a fearsome reputation as a torturer, enforcer and killer, and he rarely needed any help from anyone. Which meant that the message was loud and clear to Vincent. He would have been wary enough if H. Diller had turned up alone; to be accompanied by someone who looked just as hard meant that feathers had been ruffled and this was real business. Patience had worn out.

'H. Diller,' Vincent said, offering his hand to the black man and addressing him in the way Diller demanded. Everyone was obliged to call him H. Diller – with the exception of one man. Few people knew what the H stood for, and his insistence on it being used was nothing more than an affectation, but it was one everybody respected.

Diller smiled warmly, a smile that often lured in unsuspecting mortals. He took Vincent's hand and they shook simply, no fancy fist-banging, finger-wrapping, high-fiving, just a simple manly hand-shake. 'Jack, my son.'

There was an uncertain hesitation before Vincent spoke. 'So what brings you to these parts – these cold parts?'

'Hey, really is cold up here. Any chance of a warm?' Diller gestured to the cabin. 'We can talk in there.'

'You've come to talk?'

'You bet your soul,' Diller winked.

'Not much warmer inside.'

'Yeah, but more convivial.'

'Who's the running partner?' Vincent asked, nodding at the unsmiling man lounging by the four-wheel drive.

'That's Haltenorth. He's new, but useful.' Diller clicked his tongue.

Vincent shrugged. 'OK. There's a kettle inside we can fire up. But only got tea. That OK?'

'Magic.'

Vincent turned and led the way. His forced smile disintegrated, knowing this was no social call. This, he knew, was purely business. Dirty business. In fact he had been expecting it, nay had engineered it, but he hadn't foreseen Diller would be the lead soldier. But then again, maybe he should have. The time for games had long since gone. Problem was, he was just slightly off balance and would have felt better if his partner had been with him. It would have made the equation much more even-handed.

'Fuck,' Vincent uttered under his breath, half expecting Diller to step up behind him and stick the barrel of a pistol against his hind-brain and blow his head off. Things really had got that far, but the fact that Diller didn't kill him was the first of his mistakes. Vincent's smile returned as he opened the cabin door and allowed Diller and Haltenorth to enter ahead of him.

'You guys want to grab a chair at the far end?' Vincent said amicably, his mind manipulating angles and possibilities because he was certain this would not end prettily.

Steve Flynn smiled winningly as he passed the two pretty female cabin crew members and boarded the flight. He had managed to book a very last minute ticket, via Adam Castle's travel agency, for a flight that would take him back to Manchester from Las Palmas. He'd had a quick discussion with Castle about leaving the island for a short period. There would be nothing lost because of the lack of work. Castle also told him that a short-term disappearance might be a good thing anyway. Rumours were already circulating that the petulant charter boat customer who Flynn had accidentally knocked unconscious was after blood – or a payoff. Flynn's absence from the island might be a good thing, Castle had suggested.

Flynn heaved his only baggage into the overhead locker and edged sideways into the middle of three seats. He looked at both his travelling companions and they studiously avoided eye contact. With a sardonic twist of his mouth, he leaned forward, struggling to take off his windjammer, which he stuffed under the seat in front of him after he'd taken out the paperback thriller he was halfway through. He found his place and continued reading about a tough guy walking into town with no ID, just the clothes he stood up in, and then kicking the crap out of the 'ornery yokels'. Completely unreal, but highly exciting. Only four and a half hours to go, he thought. Then he smiled at the prospect of seeing Cathy. Her predicament sounded iffy, even though she hadn't said very much on the phone, but he was looking forward to being with her again. She promised that somehow she would pick him up from the airport.

They walked past the desk and sat on the plastic chairs at the far end of the cabin, which were positioned in the vicinity of the tiny gas-powered heater. Vincent, too, walked past the desk, and reached for the kettle – but Diller placed a hand on his forearm and glanced up at him.

'We don't need a drink, actually.'

Vincent's fingers unravelled slowly from the kettle handle.

'Mr Cain wants his money. He's tired of waiting.'

'H,' Vincent began, his voice reasonable.

'H. Diller,' he was corrected.

'H. Diller . . . look, pal, one of my donkeys got away with it. It can't be found, but I took care of him – you can't really ask for anything more than that.'

'Mr Cain wants payment.' Diller flexed his large black fingers. To his left, Haltenorth sat forward in his chair, his fingers interlocked. His eyes were angled up at Vincent.

'I don't have payment. We were ripped off by my donkey.'

'Mule, you mean?'

'I call 'em donkeys. Thicko lowlifes. Who else would take the chance, but doombrains, i.e. donkeys?'

'I see.' Diller's eyes hadn't left Vincent's face. 'In that case, Mr Cain would like goods in exchange – at double the value.'

'Twenty grand's worth?'

'Plus interest. Make it twenty-two. Round it up to twenty-five for my inconvenience, and that of Mr Haltenorth, too.'

Vincent shook his head.

'You have that amount here. This is where the distribution starts.'

'I have no stock. The vehicles took the last of it on their last run.' Vincent sighed. 'This won't go away will it, H. Diller?'

'Be like an elephant in your brain until it's settled.'

Vincent ran a hand over his unshaven face. 'I've got a grand in the petty cash drawer.' He jerked his head in the direction of the desk. Then he bent forward, placed his hands on his knees like he was going to play pat-a-cake, and looked directly into Diller's eyes. He spoke tauntingly. 'And that's all the fucker is having. That's the bill paid. It's just one of those write-offs you occasionally have to make in this business. People get greedy. That greedy person has been dealt with and that's the end of the matter – you tell him that.' Vincent rose to his full height. He wasn't a tall man, five-nine, but he was lean, with power behind his shoulders. 'I'll get you the money.'

He stepped to the desk and, as he expected, Diller moved – quickly. He shot up from the plastic chair and manoeuvred himself into a position between Vincent and the desk. At the same time, a handgun appeared in his right hand, a 9mm pistol of Chinese origin. Even with the gun jammed in the soft part underneath the cleft of his chin, Vincent recognized the weapon as part of a consignment he'd brought in and distributed two years before, one of his other sidelines. He wondered how many jobs it had been used on, how many lives it had taken, how much cash it had generated.

'N-no, back away, pal,' Diller said.

Vincent tried to swallow, his throat rising and falling against the 'O' of the muzzle. He moved as requested.

'Check the drawers,' Diller said out of the corner of his mouth. Haltenorth was already on his feet. Diller pushed Vincent further back as the other man swooped to the desk and yanked open the drawers. He rifled through them, found nothing but papers and a money tin with a piece of paper taped to it that said 'Petty Cash'.

He took it out and showed Diller.

'What did you expect, a shooter?' Vincent asked.

Diller removed the muzzle from Vincent's neck, but couldn't resist dragging the barrel up to his temple and pressing it hard against his skull, before withdrawing.

'How much in tin?' Diller asked.

'Twelve hundred, give, take,' Vincent shrugged, his face taut with tension.

'Unlock it.'

Vincent edged out of Diller's proximity and sat down on the office chair. Diller and Haltenorth stood back to watch him. He fished a key out of his jeans pocket and inserted it into the lock of the box, which measured about six inches by nine, maybe four inches deep. As he did this, his knee touched the shotgun strapped underneath the desk. His mind whirled as he worked out his moves. The flaw in it all was the time it would take him to free it from the Velcro straps, turn, rise, aim it – the weapon was ready to fire, loaded with two twelve-bore cartridges – and take out two very streetwise individuals, one of whom already had a gun in his hand. No doubt the other was also armed but hadn't yet shown his fire-power. But they had expected to find a gun in the desk drawer, and hadn't. Vincent could tell they'd dropped their guard. They'd relaxed. And that was all to his advantage. Plus they hadn't killed him yet.

'Why don't you two guys sit back down?'

'Nah, we'll stand, because it won't be enough. We had specific instructions, Jack. Oh yeah, don't get me wrong, we'll take the money – but you're still gonna die. You had your chances, y'see. That was the last one and you didn't come good.'

Vincent slowly unlocked the money box, opened the hinged lid. It was stuffed with cash, many notes, all tightly rolled up. He removed the money from the tin, a bitter expression on his face, and bounced it on the palm of his hand. 'How much to pay you guys off?' he asked, playing the game.

'What you mean?' Diller demanded.

'How much for you to go back to Cain and tell him I wasn't here, you couldn't find me? Eh?' His eyebrows arched.

Haltenorth checked out Diller, but the latter kept his eyes on Vincent, who continued with his subterfuge, because there was no way he would think about paying these guys off. 'Follow me back down to my house. I got a couple more grand stashed away. You guys take this' – he held up the money roll in his fist – 'as a show of my good will, and I'll give you the cash down at my house. Three grand, plus, in total. Not bad for a ride out to the back of beyond. It'll give me more time to get stuff together. Do me now and Cain won't be getting anything. How about it? Take the cash,' he pleaded. 'No one will be any the wiser.'

His eyes darted between the two men. He could sense Haltenorth
was up for it, but Diller wasn't even wavering.

'Mr Cain will still get his dues, man,' Diller said, 'even with you
dead. We'll just move on to your partner in crime. I'm given a job
to do, I do it.'

Haltenorth's bottom lip dropped with disappointment. Clearly he
wasn't being paid anything like the money Vincent was offering
now. Haltenorth had no loyalty in his bones. Vincent had placed
doubt in his mind.

'What about it, man?' Haltenorth hissed to Diller.

Diller turned slowly to him, unable to believe his ears. His gun
drooped to one side and his face showed complete surprise.

'I'll tell you why, dumb-ass. You do not double cross Mr Cain.
He don't do double crossing. That's why!'

'But man, all that cali.'

'I thought you were cool, man.' Diller crashed his gun across the
side of Haltenorth's head, sending him spinning backwards.

Vincent watched the short verbal exchange intently, saw the minute
change in Diller's body language that reflected his disbelief in what
he was hearing, then saw the gun arc across his dim partner's head.
Even as the gun started to move, Vincent reached under the desk
and slid the hanging shotgun out swiftly and neatly. It was a movement he had practised time and again whilst sitting at the desk. He
spun on the chair just as Haltenorth stumbled backwards, holding
the side of his bloodied head. Diller was angled slightly away from
him, the gun in his hand pointing upwards and away from Vincent.

It was a side-by-side double-barrelled sawn-off shotgun. A simple
weapon. Vincent liked simplicity, because it rarely went wrong.
Revolvers rarely went wrong, but sometimes pistols did. Sometimes
pump-action shotguns that needed racking went wrong because their
mechanisms jammed. But a simple, old-fashioned, pre-loaded one,
safety catch off, never went wrong. The only drawback was that
there were only two cartridges in it and he had to get this right first
time. He would not be allowed the privilege of reloading.

But here, in the confines of the cabin, with two targets less than
six feet away from him, he had absolute confidence that he would
be successful. He couldn't miss. The trick was to ensure that he
brought the two men down. There was the possibility they wouldn't
be killed straight away, but if they weren't dead they would be
severely injured enough that he would have time to reload.

As he spun on the chair, he held the shotgun at the base of his belly, just above the groin, angled upwards.

Diller's face turned, a scream coming to his wide mouth as he tried to spin back and bring his gun around on Vincent.

Vincent released the first barrel, the recoil thumping his tensed stomach muscles. The pellets exploded out with a huge bang and splattered across Diller's upper torso, chest, neck and head. The cartridge wad hit his throat, punching a hole in it the side of a ten pence piece. The impact hurled him against the cabin wall like a stunt man on a rope.

Vincent rose, aimed the shotgun again. Haltenorth, already stunned from the pistol whip across his head, held out his left hand beseechingly. 'No, man, no,' he cried.

Callously, Vincent shot him too.

FIVE

Henry dropped unsteadily from the bar stool but kept his balance. Donaldson emerged from the gents' toilet, wiping his mouth and walking towards Henry in a less than straight line across the pub. Henry watched him with a slightly warped grin.

'You OK, pal?'

'Yup.'

The pub had closed an hour ago and all the customers, barring Henry and Donaldson, had left. The pair had been invited up to the bar by Clayson, the landlord, where he plied them with a couple of extra pints each and a few chasers.

That meant they had each downed five pints plus numerous spirits. Henry held it quite well, whereas the American did not. He had allowed himself too many that night and it was taking its toll.

There had been times during the evening when Henry's little voice of reason told him that any over-indulgence was not a great idea. In the morning they planned to get out into the hills and do their walking trip and a skinful the night before was not the greatest of ideas. But his little devil was seduced by the ambience of the pub, the excellent taste of the beer – Clayson was proud to bursting over his clean pipes – and, of course, the offer of free drink. Their defences were well and truly weakened. They had planned to be in bed at Henry's house by eleven, but by the time they bade farewell to the landlord, who was even drunker than they were, it was quarter past midnight.

As the extremely cold night hit them, Henry staggered back a pace and Donaldson almost fell over.

'Just whoa there,' the American said as though he was steadying a stallion.

'You OK?' Henry asked him again.

'Yup . . . nope.' He walked unsteadily over to a low wall by the car park and was copiously sick.

At the same time as Karl Donaldson was emptying the contents of his stomach, Steve Flynn's flight from Las Palmas touched down at Manchester Airport. It had been uneventful. He had read his book, nodded off a few times, visited the loo and not spoken to the people either side of him. A fairly typical flight.

Although the plane docked right up to the airport terminal, Flynn could instantly feel the biting cold British night air as he stepped off the plane and entered the building via the walkway.

With no luggage to collect, he went straight out through the green channel, nothing to declare. On the flight he'd bought a bottle of Glenfiddich but had nothing customs would be interested in. He sauntered into the arrivals hall and made his way to the overhead meeting board, expecting to see Cathy.

She wasn't there.

Using his height he scanned around, but couldn't spot her. Frowning, he wandered around the terminal for a few minutes and even stepped out into the night to check outside. He knew she liked an occasional cigarette and thought she may have sneaked out for a drag.

There was no sign of her.

He resisted the temptation to have her paged. Instead he switched on his mobile phone and waited for the signal to be picked up, expecting a text or voice message from her. Nothing landed.

After fifteen further minutes, still nothing.

After half an hour the arrivals lounge was virtually empty. Flynn stood alone, looking slightly forlorn under the sign, like he'd been stood up. Thinking he had given her enough time either to call him and explain why she was late, or actually turn up flustered and apologetic, he called her. It went straight through to the answering service. Then he called the landline number she had given him. After half a dozen rings, that too clicked on to answerphone.

Cathy's pre-recorded voice came on the line. 'Hello, this is the police office at Kendleton, Lancashire. I'm PC Cathy James, your rural beat officer. I'm sorry I can't take your call right now, but if you leave a message after the tone, I promise I'll get back to you as soon as possible. If you're calling with an emergency, please hang up and redial 999.'

The tone beeped. Flynn hesitated, but hung up without saying anything. He thumbed his end-call button, a very strange, uneasy sensation in his gut. He knew Cathy well enough to be sure that if she said she would be here to pick him up, she would be. And if she wasn't, there would be one hell of a reason why not.

One hell of a bad reason, Flynn thought.

He spun on his heels and trotted over to a car rental desk, just in time to catch the booking clerk who was just about to pack up for the night. He gave the tired-looking woman his best smile and said, 'I need to hire a car, please.'

SIX

Squinting unsurely at Donaldson, Henry pursed his lips. The big American looked pale and ill. Henry knew he had spent some time both on and over the toilet overnight.

'You sure you're OK?'

'Yeah, I'm fine,' he said shortly. He hitched a medium-sized rucksack on to his back and stamped his feet. He didn't look fine, certainly not up to a five to six hour hike across the moors of Lancashire.

'We can do this another day, if you wish,' Henry persisted.

'Said I'm fine. Just had too much to drink, that's all. Once I get walking, I'll get it out of my system.'

Henry backed off and swung his own rucksack over his shoulders, securing the straps comfortably. He squatted slightly and leaned into the driver's window of his Mondeo, in which sat his wife, Kate. Behind Henry's Ford was Donaldson's excessively large four-by-four Jeep driven by Karen, his heavily pregnant wife. The two women had kindly consented to drive the men up to the starting point of their proposed hike, then take one of the cars to the finishing point at Kirkby Lonsdale, park it up and leave it for them to pick up when they finally got to their destination after two days of walking.

'Thanks for this, babe,' Henry cooed. He realized he would never have been able to do this 'guy thing' with Donaldson without Kate's – or come to that, Karen's – blessing. He had only managed to convince her by taking her away on a delayed holiday to Venice, which he had secretly extended to include four days in Tuscany, supplemented by the subtle use of flowers, the completion of chores and a lot of lurv. He knew she wasn't fooled by the sudden surge of attention, but it seemed to work. He leaned in and kissed her.

At the Jeep, Donaldson was doing much the same thing. 'You gonna be OK, baby-doll?' he said, leaning through the driver's window. He reached in and lovingly patted the ever-expanding bulge that was her third, unexpected but eagerly awaited child. 'And you too, blob.'

'We'll be fine,' she assured him. 'But you look really pale.'

'I'm OK. You know me and alcohol don't mix.' They kissed lingeringly, tongues and all. As a couple they'd had a rocky road to travel over the last few years, but that was now behind them. They were as passionately in love with each other as they had ever been.

The men stood back and the women gave waves and kisses before the cars pulled away from the side of the road, leaving primitive man to his own devices. They waved until the cars disappeared over the hill.

'Good,' Donaldson said. 'Now they're gone, let's end this charade and call a cab to take us to Blackpool for a night of debauchery.'

Henry chuckled. 'I think they would have seen through that ruse.'

'Mm, maybe.'

They surveyed their surroundings. They had been dropped off slap-bang in the centre of the Trough of Bowland, that remarkable chunk of wild countryside that forms the part of Lancashire between Lancaster and the Yorkshire Dales National Park. The intention was to walk across the Forest of Bowland, keeping due north until they reached the town of Kirkby Lonsdale. Henry estimated that, taking it reasonably easy, the journey would take two days with an overnight stop in the pretty village of Kendleton where they had booked a couple of rooms in the only pub in the village, the Tawny Owl. Henry, who had pored over maps and footpaths, estimated they would need to spend about six hours on foot each day, crossing terrain that varied from easy to difficult, but he knew both of them were well capable of completing the walk.

Henry had got back to keeping himself fit by doing a three-mile run each lunchtime with a couple of weekly bouts of circuit training. He'd lost some poundage, down to about thirteen and a half stone, and was feeling pretty fit. He knew Donaldson was a bit of a fitness freak anyway, often pounding the London pavements as well as doing a lot of weights in the state-of-the-art gym at the American embassy where he was based.

The only thing that might cause them problems was the weather. Initially it had been their intention to do the walk in autumn but because neither of them could marry up their diaries, it had dragged on until early December. Henry had made the unilateral decision that the walk would go ahead, even when Kate had warned him of the possibility of rotten weather. Henry had checked records and pooh-poohed her concerns. Winters had been mild for a long time now – 'Global warming,' he'd said knowledgeably. The worst that might happen was that they would get wet.

As the two vehicles disappeared towards Dunsop Bridge, Henry made a quick mental checklist and was happy he'd brought along everything he needed for the walk, including a change of clothing and spare trainers for the evening in the pub, which was supposed to be a great, old-fashioned hostelry. He adjusted the strap on his rucksack again, pulled his bob cap down over his ears, then set off across the road to the opening of a public footpath. The sign at the stile pointed to Brennand Tarn. Henry climbed over, flexing his toes in his recently acquired, but worn in, walking boots. As he dropped on to the other side he turned, expecting Donaldson to be right behind him, but he was still on the opposite side of the road – and had just been sick again on the grass verge.

'Bloody hell, you sure you can do this?' Henry called. 'We can get the ladies back if you want.' He held up his mobile phone and waggled it enticingly.

Donaldson wiped his mouth. 'Nahh, fine now. That was the last of it,' he said as he jogged across the road and vaulted the stile spectacularly.

Henry slid the phone back into his jacket pocket, but not before he noticed it wasn't picking up any signal.

*   *   *

'Thanks, I owe you one.' Steve Flynn rubbed his tired eyes as at 8.15 that morning he padded into the kitchen where his ex-wife, Faye, was swilling dishes at the sink. She glanced over her shoulder and gave him the up-curved smile that once, years before, had melted his heart.

He'd had a bit of a panic at the airport when Cathy had failed to show or respond to any of his calls and he was at a bit of a loss as to where he could bed down for the night. Having had to pay for car hire, his money had immediately dwindled and to get a room at an airport hotel was out of the question. Based on the flimsy fact that relations with Faye had thawed over the last few months, he took a chance and called her.

She had been groggy with sleep and part of him thought that most of the conversation he'd had with her didn't register. But when he arrived at her house – formerly *their* house – in a decent part of South Shore in Blackpool, the front door had been left unlocked and a pillow and some bedding dumped on the settee in the front room. He'd helped himself to a cheeky smidgen of whisky before settling down and dropping off to sleep almost immediately.

'No problem,' Faye said. 'Good job I wasn't entertaining a man friend, though.' As the words came out, her contrite expression told Flynn that the words were instantly regretted. Yet a pang of annoyance still shot through him. A big part of their past marital problems had been the fact that she entertained a man friend, namely Flynn's best mate and cop partner, an affair carried on behind his back for a long time.

Faye saw the cloud pass over his face and went on quickly, 'Anyway, what's going on? How come you're over here?'

He settled himself at the kitchen table. 'You remember Cathy Turnbull? Became Cathy James when she married a jack up in Lancaster?'

Faye frowned, then said, 'Oh, yeah.' She had no idea that Flynn and Cathy had had a brief fling all those years ago at the training centre. Flynn wasn't about to enlighten her.

'She was a mate, wasn't she?' Faye said, no hidden knowledge behind the words.

'Yep.' Flynn then explained Cathy's strange phone calls, but before he could finish his story, a deep male voice behind him said, 'I thought I heard you talking.'

Flynn spun. It was his son, Craig. Now fifteen years old, broadening out, shooting up, voice deepening, and on his way to becoming a bloody good-looking young man.

'Pal!' Flynn stood up and opened his arms, embracing the lad tenderly. 'Jeepers, you've grown.' They hadn't seen each other in a few months and the teenager had noticeably expanded, but in a good, healthy way.

'What are you doing here, Dad?'

'Flying visit – and your mum was good enough to let me crash out here at short notice.'

Faye watched the two of them with a proud, sad smile. Flynn caught her eye, grinned back. 'Can I take him to school?' he asked.

'Be my guest. What do you want for breakfast?'

'Has the menu changed?' Flynn knew that the kitchen wasn't Faye's most comfortable environment. She shook her head, again with that slightly crooked, heart-melting grin, taking no offence from Flynn's slight mockery. 'I'll have toast then.'

'Toast it is.'

Craig watched the exchange between the adults, his eyes narrowing. 'You guys getting back together?' he asked with cautious hope.

'Only when hell freezes over,' Faye declared and popped two slices of bread into the toaster.

Although extremely cold, the day had started bright and free of cloud, even though the wind was biting in its intensity. The two men trudged up into the Forest of Bowland, their faces into the wind, their bodies angled against it. Had this really been a forest there would have been some protection against the elements, but Bowland was only called a forest because it was once a royal hunting estate. Now it was wide open grouse moors and outcrops of millstone grit, and was designated an area of outstanding beauty.

The walk they had chosen to undertake wasn't too foolhardy, though. In his younger days Henry had roamed these moors frequently, as well as the Lake District, and the route he and Donaldson had plumped for was one Henry had walked a few times many years before. Walking was something he'd grown out of, but he still had vivid memories of crossing an unspoilt area and seeing some of the wildest scenery in the UK.

Henry was a few yards ahead of Donaldson, walking on nothing more than a narrow sheep trail, in places quite boggy. Henry's leg had sunk to mid-shin at one point and Donaldson had helped him slurp it out. Fortunately he was wearing gaiters and his foot stayed dry.

Henry stopped, his cheeks red with effort and the chill, waited for his friend to catch up. They had made slow but reasonable progress, had passed Brennand Tarn and were now making their way to Whitendale Hanging Stones.

'You OK, bud?' Henry asked, feeling it was a question he had posed many times that morning.

Donaldson still looked ill and Henry felt a little bit guilty, but, he reasoned, he had given Donaldson the opportunity to withdraw from the walk a couple of times and he'd refused.

'Yeah, yeah.'

'Fit to go on?'

'Yes,' he said firmly.

'Thing is, once we reach the stones, that's about halfway, then it's as broad as it is long.'

'I get you.' Donaldson took a mouthful from a bottle of water and wiped his lips. Henry watched him. Donaldson winced.

'Sure you're OK?'

'Yeah, just a bit of wind, I guess. I'll fart it out.'

'Let's push on.' It was 8.45 a.m., and the day had only just started.

The last time Flynn had taken Craig to school was over five years before, when the lad had been nine or ten and at junior school. He had always enjoyed the experience, watching Craig run through the school gates. Now, though, Craig was no longer a kid and when Flynn dropped him off, there was just a fleeting wave as he went to stand with a group of his pals at the school gates. Flynn watched him for a few moments, bursting with pride, before pulling away into the four-wheel-drive traffic outside the school. At least his union with Faye had produced one good thing.

He drove back to Faye's house. She had gone to work and had told him he could use the place if he needed a shower, which he did. He wandered slowly through the rooms, seeing how little had actually changed in the years he'd been excluded from the place. The dining room was still how he had decorated it, and so was the master bedroom. Craig's room had been repainted and the main bathroom completely refitted. Flynn recalled that was an insurance job after a leak had caused a lot of damage when Faye had been away.

He undressed, showered and shaved in the en suite shower room off the main bedroom. He sat on the edge of the unmade bed after, drying himself off, when a surge of tiredness pulsed through him. He lay back and closed his eyes, thinking he would rest for a few minutes.

Half an hour later he jumped awake, cursing. He dressed quickly, using the underwear he had brought along in the flight bag, keeping on the jeans and shirt he'd worn the day before. Then he called Cathy on her mobile. It went directly to answerphone, frustratingly, as did the landline number she had given him.

He stood by the kitchen window overlooking the compact, over-grown back garden, a mug of tea in his hand. His mouth crimped in thought. He looked down at his mobile phone, weighing it all up, then decided to make another call, just on the off chance. He tabbed through the contacts menu, found the name he was after, pressed the green dial button with his thumb and put the phone to his ear.

'Can I help you?'

'I take it you don't introduce yourself and your department for the sake of secrecy?' Flynn said.

'As I said, can I help you?'

'Jerry, my old cocker, how the hell've you been, matey?'

For a moment it was as if the line had gone dead. Then, 'What the hell do you want?'

'You sound cautious, maybe not even pleased to hear from me,' Flynn chuckled.

'Last time I spoke to you, I ended up telling you things I shouldn't have. Got me in the shit with my boss,' DC Jerry Tope whined.

'Ahh, Henry Christie? How is the twat?'

There was another pause. 'What do you want, Steve?'

'First of all, for you not to worry. What I need to know won't compromise you this time.' Flynn smiled to himself. 'Unless of course you don't tell me, in which case I'll have to make a very delicate phone call . . . if you get my drift? How is the lovely Marina, by the way?'

'Flynn, you're the twat.'

Flynn cackled wickedly. He had known Jerry Tope for a very long time and they had been good friends when Flynn had been a cop in Lancashire Constabulary. So good that Flynn had done Tope a great favour once, lying to save Tope's marriage. Ever since, Tope had been in Flynn's debt. Flynn had never expected to become a debt collector but he had tapped into Tope's role as an intelligence analyst the previous year when he was after some details of a couple of very bad men who were out to get him. Their friendship had not survived Flynn's ignominious departure from the cops, but Flynn had found it useful to have someone on the inside who could search databases.

'It's different this time,' Flynn said.

'I seriously doubt it.'

'Honest – Cathy James? You remember her. Cathy Turnbull as was?'

'Yeah, we were all at training school together. Everybody wanted to get into her panties. Rumour had it that someone did . . .'

'Yeah, lucky sod, whoever it was.'

'You did, didn't you!' Tope exclaimed. 'Jeez, you did. Now it all fits into place. Christ, if I'd known that,' he said wistfully.

'I didn't, actually,' Flynn lied. 'But, yeah, Cathy James, née Turnbull.'

'Mm, haven't come across her for years. Do know she's working a rural beat up in Northern Division. She married a jack from Lancaster. Tom James, good lad.'

'Know much about him?'

'No, just of him. Good thief-taker by all accounts. Used to be a traffic cop, of all things, but seems to have found his niche. I think Henry's used him a few times on murders. And he recently got a chief cons commendation for busting a prostitution racket. Probably go far . . . Look, why?'

'Oh, nothing. It's just that I'm here on a flying visit and thought I'd drop in on Cathy.'

'You're back in Lancashire?' Tope said it as though Flynn's presence was something akin to a deadly virus.

'Affirmative.'

'Ugh. Why don't you just call her up?'

'Done – no reply.'

Jerry Tope sighed. 'Hold on, I'll check the duty states.' Flynn heard the tap of his fingers on a keyboard, Tope accessing the computerized system that recorded the working hours of every officer on duty within Lancashire. 'You back for good?' Tope asked.

'As I said, flying visit.'

'Good . . . here we are . . . she's down as being on a rest day today. Maybe she's gone out for the day.'

'What about Tom?'

More key-tapping. 'Nine-five,' which Flynn knew meant nothing as far as detectives were concerned. They tended to be loose about what hours they actually worked and the official system was often wrong. 'Oh, what about yesterday?'

'Yesterday? Um, Cathy, rest day, Tom, nine-five.'

'Thanks, Jerry.'

'That it?'

'Uh-huh.'

'Thank God for small mercies.'

Flynn hung up feeling ever so slightly guilty, but not so much that he wouldn't use Tope's knowledge and position again if necessary. Because there was no statute of limitations on adultery, Flynn's knowledge of Tope's one and only infidelity was something he would hold over him for the rest of his life.

He scribbled a note to Faye, thanking her for letting him crash out and use her facilities, left twenty pounds he could ill afford for Craig, collected his gear and locked the house, then jumped into his hire car. He hoped that he would be done with whatever problem was ailing Cathy by tomorrow and was already looking forward to going home to Gran Canaria, even if he was going to be sued for assault by the jumped-up Hugo. He was missing the feel of the boat under his feet and even though *Faye 2* was going to be in dry dock for a couple of months, he wanted to be there, tending her, carrying out any necessary repairs and in general looking after his baby. Survival money would come from somewhere.

'This is the centre of the known world,' Henry Christie said grandly as he swung his rucksack off his shoulder and sat down on the ugly rocky boulders busting out of the heathland that were known as Whitendale Hanging Stones. 'Well,' he said, amending the claim as he delved into the rucksack for his steel flask and sandwiches, 'the middle of Britain, anyway.'

He unscrewed the flask and poured himself a welcome coffee, sipping it as he admired the view from a vantage point that made him feel on top of the world.

'Whaddya mean?' Donaldson said indifferently. He dropped his rucksack beside Henry, sat down miserably and pulled his anorak hood over his head.

Henry looked at him, realizing what the term 'green at the gills' meant. Donaldson was not improving healthwise. If anything, he looked more unwell than earlier and it had been his excellent physical condition that had kept him going up to this point. They had been walking for three hours and when the sheep tracks had petered out, it had been tough going. The bogs were unforgiving and possibly treacherous to the unwary.

'I mean that this position here is the geographical centre of the British Isles – if the four hundred and one outlying islands are included in the calculation.'

'Oh.' Donaldson sounded unimpressed. He had food and drink in his rucksack, but did not open up and get any, just sat there glumly.

It was very windy at this location, 496 metres above sea level, and icy blasts seared through their layers of clothing.

Henry sipped his hot coffee and bit into a Lancashire cheese sandwich, laced with piccalilli, as he surveyed the countryside. It was a truly magnificent vista, the hills of Bowland and Pendle lying like huge sleeping dinosaurs. He looked at the sky. To the south it was fairly clear, and across to the west he could still make out the pinprick that was Blackpool Tower on the coast. He swivelled around, then his eye caught a bird zooming across the moorland just below him. A frisson of joy shot through him.

'Would you look at that?'

In his not misspent youth, Henry had been a bit of a birdwatcher and could still recognize most of the common species, as well as many birds of prey, which were always a favourite. And what he saw made his heart beat faster with excitement. An adult male hen harrier, grey plumage above, white underneath, showing its dark wing-tips as it shot past. It was a rare bird and still persecuted by ruthless gamekeepers.

Donaldson didn't even look up, but said, 'What?'

'Nothing.'

'Ooh.' Donaldson hissed and doubled up, gripping his stomach. He scrambled to his feet, gave Henry a desperate look, and ran behind a rocky outcrop.

Henry looked to the north-east. The sight he saw filled him with some dread. Maybe thirty miles distant, the clouds were black, rolling and heavy. 'Not good,' he said.

A few moments later, Donaldson reappeared, his complexion grey. 'You OK?' Henry asked him again.

'I've just had the shits on the middle of Britain,' he said.

Flynn had driven out of Blackpool and dropped on to the M55, heading east across Lancashire. At the junction with the M6, he bore left and north, eventually passing Lancaster on his left, then the young offenders' institution, exiting the motorway at junction 34. Then he'd gone right, heading in a vague north-easterly direction along the A683, following the Lune valley, the River Lune being Lancashire's second river after the Ribble. He passed through the village of Caton, past the police house on the left, but before he reached the next settlement, Hornby, he took a right turn, picking up the signs for Low and High Bentham, then took another right following the sign for Kendleton.

The tight meandering roads rose steadily and at one point on the brow of a hill, he got a superb view of the hills across the Yorkshire Dales National Park in the next county.

The view was marred only by the approaching black sky – and if he wasn't mistaken, Flynn was certain that flecks of snow were in the air. He cursed and thought of the magnificent weather he'd left behind, two thousand miles to the south.

SEVEN

The black Range Rover with smoked-out windows loomed large in Flynn's rear view mirror. His hire car, a tiny Peugeot, had been the only vehicle on the road for the last four miles in any direction, but the big four-wheel drive had come up behind quickly and unexpectedly and almost attached itself to Flynn's rear bumper. The road was narrow, widening very occasionally, but virtually impossible for overtaking, which is what the driver of the Range Rover obviously wanted to do.

The headlights flashed repeatedly but Flynn had nowhere to go, nowhere to pull off. On both sides of the road were either very

spongy looking grass verges or deep drainage channels. Maybe if
he pulled in tight and slowed right down, the Range Rover might
be able to pass carefully.

Flynn's eyes constantly checked the mirror, which was now
completely filled with the front radiator grille of the following car.
He gritted his teeth and began to seethe as the driver kept up the
pressure on him. He had been just tootling up to that point, but the
harrying from behind made him increase speed involuntarily.

And then reduce it. He wasn't going to be intimidated by some
clown in a fancy motor. If the guy wanted to pass so badly, go
ahead, welcome, and don't blame me if you end up in a field. But
Flynn wasn't going to accommodate him by sinking his own wheels
into a muddy verge, or worse running into a ditch.

'Wanker,' he breathed.

The guy didn't let up, kept pushing.

Flynn's hands gripped the wheel white-knuckle tight, still nowhere
to pull in and let the car pass.

And then the inevitable happened.

Coming out of a right-hand corner, Flynn saw another car coming
towards him, a Jeep or something, a similar size to the one clinging
to his rear end. Whatever happened, this was going to be a squeeze.

Flynn had to jam on the brakes on the narrow road, which was
just about wide enough for two standard-sized cars to pass carefully.
He slowed right down, as did the approaching Jeep. Two cars
approaching each other on a country road, the drivers showing
courtesy towards each other. And behind him the impatient Range
Rover.

Flynn signalled his intention to pull in.

But then the Range Rover swerved out and accelerated past,
taking off his driver's door mirror with a loud crack. Flynn jumped.

The Range Rover powered ahead, its offside wheels leaving tracks
in the opposite bank and forcing the oncoming Jeep to veer left and
on to that same bank with its nearside wheels. The Range Rover
sped past, this time taking the driver's door mirror of the Jeep and
avoiding a scraping collision by what seemed only millimetres to
Flynn.

And then, with a gush of exhaust smoke, it was gone, leaving
him and the Jeep stationary, facing each other.

Flynn could see a woman at the wheel, another in the passenger
seat. Leaving his engine running, he climbed out of the Peugeot

and examined the door and the remnants of the damaged mirror which had been jaggedly snapped off. Broken bits of it, including shattered glass, were scattered on the road. He picked up the biggest piece, kicked a few other scraps of plastic and metal off the road and walked to the Jeep, seeing the debris of that vehicle's door mirror strewn down the road.

Flynn had taken off his jacket to drive and was in short sleeves. The brutally cold wind pierced his bones as he reached the Jeep. The driver's door window opened slowly, revealing the woman at the wheel.

'Are you all right?' he asked.

'Yeah, yeah, reckless sod. Are you?'

'Yeah. He'd been up my chuffer for a mile or two but I couldn't find anywhere to pull in.' He bent his knees and looked into the Jeep across at the woman in the passenger seat. 'Are you unhurt?'

She nodded. 'Thanks.'

Both were very attractive and neither seemed unduly frightened by their experience. Cool women, he thought.

'Did you get his number?' the woman at the wheel asked.

He nodded and tapped his head. 'Up here.'

'Don't suppose there'll be much point in pursuing it,' she said.

'Probably not. Mine's a hire car, so I'll have to pass on details to the company and report it to the police. It was a hit and run after all. Anyway, if I give you my details and you give me yours, maybe we could be witnesses for each other if it comes to it? Whether you want to tell your insurance company or the cops is up to you, but I don't want to get saddled with a bill I can't afford to pay. What d'you say?'

'Good idea.' She fished out a pad and pen, handed it to Flynn. He jotted down his details and the registered number of the Range Rover. He gave Faye's address as his own. Didn't want to get too complicated by bringing Gran Canaria into the equation. He handed the pad back and she wrote down her name and a mobile number. Moments later both vehicles were back on the road.

Flynn discovered that Kendleton was actually not much more than a hamlet. As he drove into it he guessed there was probably no word to describe something that fell between a village and a hamlet. 'A hamage?' he mused. Whatever, it was a picturesque little place. To its credit, it had a nice-looking pub called the Tawny Owl which advertised en suite rooms, but as he drove past, he saw a 'No

Vacancies' sign propped up in a window. There was a shop-cum-post office, a few houses scattered around a tiny village green and a babbling brook fed by water coming down off Great Harlow, the hill that dominated the village to the south. There was also a butcher's shop and amazingly, a red telephone box that looked as though it had not been vandalized.

Within seconds he had driven through, then the road rose steeply again and after about half a mile, he came to the red-brick detached police house/office in which Cathy James lived and from which she performed her role as rural beat officer for the area.

Flynn remembered a conversation he'd had with Cathy years before in which she had declared her undying passion for animals and nature. Her ambition was either to be a dog handler or a member of the mounted branch, or a wildlife officer, or, failing all of them, a rural beat officer. She had become a dog handler quite early in her service but it had been her failed marriage to another dog handler that put paid to her career in that department. His mates on the branch had given her an underhanded hard time and eventually she'd had enough and managed to move on to the mounted branch, where she had a few good, enjoyable years with a massive piece of sweaty flesh trapped between her legs. Lucky horse, Flynn thought dreamily, pulling up outside the house.

Following mounted she had got the job as rural beat officer here in Kendleton, the biggest beat in Lancashire, covering a wild, sparsely populated area. Her job included a lot of wildlife conservation and enforcement. Poachers, she'd once told Flynn, were a dangerous menace.

Flynn opened the car door a crack. The harsh wind from the upper moors rushed in and almost ripped it out of his hand with its strength. There was more snow in the air now, beginning to fall thickly with the possibility of sticking. Flynn put his jacket on and was about to open the door again, but a sixth sense made him check over his shoulder just in time and slam it shut again as the same black Range Rover that had ripped off his door mirror shot past less than three feet away. It carried on up the hill and disappeared over the crest into the encroaching weather.

'Gonna get you,' Flynn promised grimly. This time he made sure nothing was coming before getting out and walking up the driveway, past a selection of bushes and trees, to the front door of Cathy's house. From inside he heard the sound of a barking dog.

'Like I said before, it's as broad as it's long,' Henry apprised Donaldson. 'Now it'll take us just as long to get back to where we started from as it will to where we're going.'

'Basically we're in the middle of nowhere,' Donaldson concluded morosely.

'Pretty much,' Henry agreed. He looked to the north-east again. The view was quickly disappearing as the black, snow-laden clouds moved quickly towards them, a bit like the devil in the film *Night of the Demon*, Henry thought. The film had scared the living daylights out of him whilst watching it on TV once, when he was a home-alone teenager. He swallowed nervously and cursed the weather forecast. There had been the possibility of snow, but it had definitely shown just a light dusting down the Northumberland coast, at least a hundred miles away from his present location. Something had gone seriously wrong in the stratosphere, he thought bleakly. A north-easterly which had probably begun life somewhere over the steppes of Russia was now blowing bitterly, and was bringing a huge blanket of snow with it.

He saw Donaldson wince again as a severe griping pain creased his guts. He had been to the toilet again – 'Shitting a fountain' had been his wonderfully evocative description of the act – and it was now apparent he was suffering from something far worse than a hangover. Diagnosis: food poisoning. Something he laid well and truly at the door of the landlord of the Tram & Tower, and its chicken-based menu to be precise.

'Musta been that chicken,' Donaldson said.

'I had chicken too,' Henry said. 'I think I'm OK.'

'Not the same dish,' Donaldson pointed out. 'Sorry pal, I need to go again.' He shot behind a rocky outcrop, out of sight, and yanked his trousers down with a long groan.

Henry's jaw rotated thoughtfully as he glanced at his mobile phone. Still no signal, which seemed ironic being at such a height above sea level. If it was food poisoning, the journey ahead was going to be tough. Henry knew how debilitating it could be, even the mildest dose. To have been stuck out here even on a sunny day would be bad enough, but, as his eyes took in the approaching weather front, this was going to be extra, extra difficult.

The snow, which had started as a sprinkle, had become much heavier, something Henry hadn't seen the likes of for twenty years.

He glanced down at his map and compass, the only items he'd thought he would need for the walk, and cursed. He had a GPS at home, thought it would be unnecessary, now wished he'd brought it along.

Donaldson emerged from cover, gave Henry a sheepish smile. 'Feel slightly better.'

'OK to push on?'

'No choice, is there? Can hardly stay up here.'

A sudden gust of wind caught the two men, almost knocking them over with its ferocity. It carried sleet with it, slashing across Henry's exposed face as though he was being pebble-dashed. It hurt. He tugged his bob cap down over his ears and pulled his jacket hood over too. He turned so his back was against the wind. Ahead was a sheep track, heading due north.

'Need to be going in that direction.' He pointed.

'Yeah, let's go, pal.'

Flynn knocked. The dog barked louder. He knocked again, bent down to the letter box and flipped it open to peer through. The whole of the rectangular gap was filled by the snout and menacing, bared, snarling teeth of a very large German shepherd dog. Flynn jumped back with a little squeal as the dog snapped nastily at him.

'Nice doggy,' he said. He took a couple of steps backwards and checked the front of the house. It had probably been built in the 1960s and was of typical design for a police house of that era, with the exception that it had been extended on one side for the office and on the other by a double garage with a bedroom above. Flynn knew that the force had done its best to get rid of all the rural beats covering far-flung countryside areas where nothing much seemed to happen and the cost of policing was disproportionate to the results achieved. The powers that be had managed to close a lot of the rural stations, but Kendleton had remained open because of vocif-erous public and parish council pressure. And the fact that Cathy did a fantastic job. She had been single – newly divorced – when she took up the post before the cost-cutting started. Within a year she had wormed her way into the heart of the community and got quantitative results as well as the touchy-feely stuff. When the force tried to close the beat down, there had been severe ructions from the tribal elders and they had to back down.

She had also done a deal to buy the house, with the promise she would continue to stay on as local beat officer. The house, considered prime real estate, had cost a fortune, but marriage to Tom, a DC in Lancaster, had eased the pain of purchase.

Flynn thought about this as he walked along the front of the house, past the huge bay window of the lounge, down the side then through the unlocked gate into the back garden. It was a massive, unkempt chunk of land. Flynn walked along the back of the house, peering into the windows, seeing no one. However, by going on tiptoe he could see into the garage and there was a car parked inside, a VW Golf. For some reason, he thought this was likely to be Tom's car. When he got back around to the front, he started knocking again, clattering the letter box and generally driving the dog bonkers.

Jack Vincent had a pen in his hands, a cheap ball-point, holding it between the thumb and first finger of both hands.

The cabin door opened and the lorry driver called Callard stepped in. He had just returned from his third delivery of aggregate of the day. His vehicle was now going through the power wash. He had done his last run.

Vincent's eyes refocused from the pen to Callard's nervous figure. 'What?'

'I want out,' Callard spluttered.

Vincent's lips twisted into a cruel grin. 'You want out? Out of what?'

'This.' He made a sweeping gesture with his hands. 'This whole fucking thing.'

Vincent looked at him for a few moments, licked his lips, then placed the pen down slowly on the desk without a sound.

'I can't do it,' Callard admitted. He'd been taking a big chance that day, knowing the cops and the ministry were out and about. The evening before he had got seriously drunk down at the village pub and had continued drinking once he got home, only flopping into bed at 4 a.m., horrendously pissed. His alarm had gone off at six, but a shower, shave and copious amounts of coffee had done nothing to alleviate his condition. So he had driven drunk and had continued to sip from a bottle of whisky throughout the day, maintaining the level.

Drinking had been Callard's problem before, the reason why no one else would touch him with a barge pole. Since Vincent had taken him on, he'd kept himself sober for the driving, but last night had tipped him over the edge again. And the reason he got drunk wasn't connected in any way to the demons that haunted his past: the divorces, the depression, money troubles, the deaths.

The reason for last night's bender was helping to clear up a blood-soaked crime scene.

Two dead black guys. One with his throat blasted out, the other with half the side of his face missing. And the fibreglass walls of the cabin splattered with blood, gore and brains.

And the shotgun had still been in Jack Vincent's hands, literally still smoking.

Callard had just been under the crusher at the quarry, refilling his lorry with hardcore, had driven to the weighbridge and was ready to get back on the road when Henderson swung up on to the footplate and leaned in the driver's window.

'We need some assistance.'

'What d'you mean?'

'Switch off, come with me.'

Callard shrugged. He got out, followed the big fitter to the cabin. Vincent was standing at the door, talking to the woman who did the admin at the other cabin. She was a wiry woman in late middle age called Penny. They stopped talking as the two men approached and Penny took a step back, angling herself to one side to let the men stand in front of Vincent. It was then that Callard noticed the shotgun hanging loosely in Vincent's right hand, at his thigh, a wisp of smoke coming from the barrel.

'Been some bother,' Vincent said. A major understatement. He stood aside. Henderson went past him, looked down the cabin, then glanced at Vincent and sniffed up.

'Crusher?' he asked efficiently.

'One of 'em, the other's cat food.'

Callard had no idea what they were talking about. 'What's going on?'

'Take a look,' Vincent gestured in a 'be my guest' kind of way.

And from Callard's reaction, Vincent knew that he was going to be a problem. Drunks always were. Untrustworthy, self-absorbed and pathetic.

Vincent now looked at his driver, having expected something like this. He wouldn't have minded, but he knew of Callard's past. There was violence in it, he'd once been a minder for a low-level drug dealer, had broken fingers in his younger days, made people squeal for mercy.

Now he was an alcohol-riddled wimp. He said, 'It's gone beyond that, Larry. You're too much a part of it now. All that drug transporting, now helping me to dispose of two bodies, one of which you took in the aggregate this morning.' He smiled at Callard, his eyes hooded. 'Accessory to murder at the very least. You're locked in, pal.'

'Jack, I won't say anything . . . I just . . .'

'Look, come in proper, don't stand there. Let's chat. This'll be OK. Seriously. No worries.'

Callard hesitated, then stepped into the cabin, his eyes quickly moving to the far back wall on which most of the flesh and blood of the dead men had been splattered. Now you couldn't tell. Once the bodies had been dragged out and disposed of, Vincent had set Callard to work with a power washer inside the cabin. As the furniture in that section was all cheap plastic, it hadn't mattered about it getting soaked. Callard had covered his wooden desk with a plastic sheet, pulled open the drain plug in the cabin floor and got to work, hosing it all away. He'd gagged at first, then gone on to autopilot. Dazed, shocked and simply doing what he'd been told to do, terrified of the consequences of refusal. The washer had done a good job and Callard had spent extra time spraying the water jets into the nooks and crannies, transfixed as the resultant liquid mix gurgled away down the plughole.

And that was after he'd helped to get rid of the bodies.

He and Henderson, who had been completely unaffected by the task, had dragged the first body all the way to the stone crusher. Henderson adjusted the machine to spew out the finest grade of rock and then they'd hauled the body on to the conveyor belt, switched it on and watched it feed in.

The second body was more of a conundrum as far as Callard was concerned. He could see the reasoning in getting rid of a body through a crusher. It was pounded to nothing. Spat out on to a pile of hardcore, then tipped into a lorry and would eventually be part of the foundations underneath the stretch of motorway the hardcore was dumped at.

No body. No evidence. A very good way of disposing of it. Even Callard could see that.

But the second body?

He and Henderson had heaved it on to the back of Vincent's Toyota four-wheel drive. Henderson drove up beyond the working quarry, on rough, deeply gouged tracks, up on to the rim of the disused quarry that Vincent also owned on the hillside behind his house. This was fenced off by a high, thick chain-link fence with many 'Danger – No Entry' signs posted on it. Henderson stopped at a gate, unlocked it and drove through, then around various tracks until they came to the old single-storey explosives store on the far edge of the quarry. Under Henderson's instructions they dragged the dead body off the flat-back and dumped it inside the store, which was about the size of a small garage.

Henderson drove back to the cabin. Callard was told it was his job to clean up the mess, then power wash the back of the Toyota too, which was smeared with blood as though they'd had the carcass of a deer in it.

All these awful memories were still vivid in Callard's brain as Vincent sat him down.

'You owe me big style,' Vincent said. 'No one else would take you on, but I did. It's not as though you didn't know what you were getting into, is it?'

Callard stared numbly at his boss. Then blurted, 'The drugs, yeah – but killing! Fuck me, Jack! You in a turf war or something?'

'Sometimes the shit hits the fan. Bad things happen and they have to be dealt with – and that's what happened here.' Vincent slid open a desk drawer, took out the money box and opened it. His hand came out with a big roll of notes crushed in his palm, the same ones he had shown the now deceased H. Diller and his equally dead backup, Haltenorth. 'But we always get good money for what we do, don't we?' He looked at the cash. 'I don't know how much there is here, but it's yours for what you did yesterday.' His hand stretched out to Callard, offering it.

'Don't want it,' he said stubbornly. 'Just want out. I can't take what's going on.'

Vincent's mouth tightened. Slowly he slid the money back into the cash tin and locked it. He pocketed the small key and rested his right hand, fingers slightly outstretched, across the box, which was just small enough for him to pick up with the one hand, like a brick. He picked it up as though he was going to replace it in the drawer.

Then he smashed it across Callard's head.

The tin wasn't particularly heavy. But it was sturdy and well constructed. It was a secure money box, after all, made of quite thick metal. The force of the blow deformed Callard's whole face for a moment and he crashed off the chair on to his hands and knees. Vincent discarded the box and reverted to his fists, pounding Callard's head until, finished, he stood up slowly and breathless. Callard scuttled away across the cabin, whimpering and groaning. Vincent stood over him.

'I decide,' he gasped, 'who comes, who stays, who goes and what you do. I own you. I decide. And you'll do everything I tell you.'

EIGHT

During his time as a cop, Flynn had hammered on many doors, especially when he'd been on the drugs branch. Somehow an instinct was acquired as to whether anyone was at home, but on this occasion it didn't take the greatest detective in the world to work out there was a reasonable chance someone was inside. The car in the garage was a bit of a clue, as was the presence of the dog. Maybe. Or maybe Tom was at work, had got a lift in, and no one was inside.

Flynn shrugged mentally. He thumped the side of his fist on the door, rattled the letter box and stuck his finger on the door bell, making enough noise to raise the dead.

They pushed against the worsening weather, heads bowed, for as they trudged northwards, the north-easterly came in at them from forty-five degrees to the right, continually buffeting them and making walking along some stretches of the narrow paths quite dangerous.

Henry led, Donaldson bringing up the rear, trapped in his own world. To the American it had all become a bit unreal and he was focused on nothing more than the function of putting one foot in front of the other and the huge effort that it took. What he wanted to do was succumb to the awful way he was feeling, the nausea that enveloped him, the pain that weakened him every time it shot across his lower guts, and the fact that he dared not even fart. He even chuckled at that thought – and then the pain wracked him again and sapped more energy. His knees were weakening all the time, his muscles beginning to feel soft and pudgy. He pushed on, hoping his physical fitness and his mental attitude would be his saviour.

Henry was maybe ten feet ahead of him, but as the sleet turned to proper snow and the wind whipped it around, it became a series of interplaying curtains in front of his eyes, making it hard to keep Henry in view.

A sudden panic came over Donaldson. He was a tough guy and had been in many life-and-death situations, but they had always been on level playing fields or, more usually, Donaldson had had the advantage. And with the exception of one major blip – when he'd come face to face with one of the world's most wanted terrorists and almost lost his life – he had always come out on top. Because he was fit, healthy, strong and hadn't eaten bad chicken the night before. He could hardly believe how terribly it was affecting him, how vulnerable it was making him feel.

Henry disappeared in a snow flurry. Donaldson shouted his name desperately.

And then he was back in sight, had turned and was waiting for him to catch up. 'Jeez, man, I thought you'd gone.'

'No mate, still here,' Henry reassured him. 'How's it going?'

Donaldson shook his head. Not good.

Persistence paid off. Flynn saw the twitch of the curtain at the bedroom window and knew for certain. He waited patiently but when the door was still not opened he began banging again, using his knuckles for a short *rat-a-tat*, often more irritating than the bass drum knock with the side of the fist.

The dog continued to bark.

There was a shout from inside the house and the dog fell silent. Flynn heard a movement, a door closing, footsteps. Then behind the frosted glass inlaid in the UPVC door he saw a shadowy figure, heard the key turn in the lock and the door opened a couple of inches on the security chain.

Tom James's face appeared at the crack, but not the clean-cut face Flynn remembered from last year's honeymoon. The eyes were sunk deep in their sockets, bleary and shot with blood. He was unshaven and even from where he stood, Flynn could smell the body odour. At knee level, the dog's long nose poked through the gap, sniffing, growling.

Tom didn't even look directly at Flynn, just said, 'What the hell d'you want?' A whiff of stale booze came to Flynn's nostrils.

Flynn hesitated. 'Tom, it's me, Steve Flynn.'

The detective's eyes rose wearily. A glint of recognition came to them, but not friendliness. He did not unlatch the chain, simply said, 'What're you doing here?' There was suspicion and challenge in the voice.

'I was over here visiting family,' Flynn fibbed. 'Just had the chance to pop over and catch up with you and Cathy. On the off chance, y'know?'

'Oh, very nice.' Tom did not budge.

'Is she about?'

Tom shook his head. 'No.'

'Right,' Flynn said, expanding the syllable to indicate disbelief. 'Er, any chance of getting a brew?' he suggested. 'It's brass out here.' He wrapped his arms around himself to prove his point and exhaled a steamy breath.

Tom considered him, put the door to and slid the chain free. 'Come in,' he said reluctantly.

'The weather's turning real nasty,' Flynn observed.

The door opened. Tom was dressed in a dressing gown over a T-shirt and shorts, slippers on his feet. He fastened the gown, grabbed the dog by its thick collar. 'He won't do you any harm once you're in,' Tom said.

Flynn edged around the dog. It eyed him malevolently. It was a massive beast and he guessed it was the one Cathy had handled whilst she'd been on the dog section. The dogs were usually allowed to stay with their handlers when they left the department if they had a long-standing partnership, for in such cases it would be too problematic to re-establish an old dog with a new handler. Always better to start afresh. The dog did look quite old, greying like a human being, and Flynn guessed it would be around the nine year mark, if he did his maths correctly. However, its eyes remained sharp and keen, watching him enter the house and turn right into the lounge.

'Nice doggy,' he said.

'His nickname was Lancon Bastard,' Tom said. 'But he's a doddering old softy now, on his last legs, literally. He's called Roger, of all things,' he added tiredly and Flynn picked up that he wasn't keen on the beast. 'Grab a seat. I'll put the kettle on.'

'Great.' Flynn sat on the settee, glancing around at the furniture and fittings in the bay-fronted room. Everything looked expensive. The soft leather three-piece suite, the forty-two-inch TV mounted on the wall over the fireplace, the surround sound to go with it, a Bang and Olufsen sound system and a series of watercolours that looked original. Through the front window he saw that the snow had thickened and stuck, already some depth to it, and he worried if he was going to be able to get out of the village today. Whilst he was thinking this, Roger was framed in the doorway, observing him.

Flynn turned his head slowly and smiled cautiously. 'Hello, Roger,' he said quietly. He could hear Tom in the kitchen, mugs being placed on work surfaces, the tap filling the kettle.

'Where's your mum, then?' Flynn asked the dog. The ears twitched, so did the tail – in a friendly way, Flynn hoped. He held out his hand warily, hoping it wouldn't be seen as a piece of meat to be chewed on. 'You going to say hello?' The dog didn't move, but the tail wagged and the ears flickered uncertainly.

Tom appeared behind the dog, placed the sole of his slipper against its back hip joint and pushed the animal roughly away. 'Shift, dimwit,' he said and came into the living room bearing two mugs. He handed one to Flynn, then sat in an armchair. The dog, cowed by the push, stayed in the hallway, looking in.

'So, Tom, how's it going? How's married life?' Flynn asked brightly.

Tom's mug had almost reached his mouth and stopped under his bottom lip as he considered the question. He looked through slitted eyes at Flynn and said, 'OK,' non-committal.

'Good, good,' Flynn said. He sipped his coppery-tasting brew. 'Where is the lass, then? Out working?'

Tom shrugged. 'Yeah, probably . . . haven't actually seen her in a couple of days . . . shifts and that . . . ships that pass in the night.'

'So you don't know where she is?' Flynn tried to phrase the question as unthreateningly as possible.

'No, I don't. I've been working a big case in Lancaster, so I've been doing all the hours that God sends. We'll collide eventually, then we'll be in each other's hair for days,' he laughed. 'That's how it is – cops who get married. Not easy.'

'Yeah, guess you're right.'

Tom looked across the room at Flynn, waiting. Flynn sipped his tea, feeling extremely uneasy. 'Look, as a friend,' he said, now trying not to sound too patronizing, 'you sure everything's OK between you?'

'Has she phoned you? Is that why you're here?' Tom snapped. Before Flynn could answer, he went on, 'Everything's fine, OK? So, nice to see you and all that, but I need to get ready to get back to work. Need a shit, shave and a shower. You finish off your tea, let yourself out. Sorry you had a wasted journey.' He rose to his feet and swept past Flynn, then up the stairs. Flynn watched him open-mouthed, then clamped his lips shut with a clash of his teeth.

The dog sat at the open door, ears back, tail swatting sideways, back and forth across the carpet behind him.

'Some people, eh?' Flynn laughed, and thought, *Definitely not the same Tom James I met last year on holiday. Maybe that's what marriage does to a person . . . hm, it did to me.*

Flynn stood up and went into the kitchen, passing within inches of Roger's big wet nose, hoping he wasn't one of those sly dogs that let you in, then refused to let you out. He swilled his mug, then came back into the hallway. Ahead of him was the front door, to the left the lounge and to the right a door marked 'Office', leading through to the police station bit of the house. He glanced upstairs. He could hear Tom moving around and the sound of a shower being turned on. He looked at the dog, still sitting in the hallway, but having swivelled around ninety degrees to keep an eye on the stranger.

'What d'you think?' he said. The dog wagged its tail. Flynn took that as a yes, so he tried the office door and found it open.

'What gets me,' Henry moaned, 'is that no matter how good and advanced technology gets, nature always has the last laugh.' He shook his mobile phone and considered lobbing the useless thing into the snow. He didn't, but was finding it increasingly frustrating that there was no signal to be had on his, or Donaldson's, phone. They were sheltering under the lee of a rocky outcrop, out of the winds that had continued to strengthen and bring thick curtains of snow with them. Donaldson was huddled beside him, unable to even mouth a response as his illness became progressively worse.

Henry had drunk the last of his coffee and taken some from Donaldson's flask, swapping the hot drink for a bottle of water, basing the transaction on the belief that it was important for Donaldson to keep his pure liquid intake up to compensate for the stuff leaving his body. Coffee wouldn't be much good for him, even though they were entering a phase that Henry thought would be a balancing act. Donaldson needed to keep up his fluids, yes, and water was the best, yes, but he also needed to keep warm as the temperature dropped, and a few mouthfuls of coffee could help that. Maybe. Coffee, though, didn't always have a beneficial effect on the bowels.

Henry finished his high-energy cereal bar that tasted of card, then stood up. The harsh wind blew into his face, so he dropped back down again, unfolded his Ordnance Survey map and tried to plot their current position using that and the woefully inadequate compass.

'Where are we?'

Henry blew out his cheeks and placed a gloved finger on the map. 'Here,' he said confidently.

Donaldson did not even glance. 'Let's push on.' He got up unsteadily, swung his rucksack on to his back, then doubled over in agony.

The office was pretty sparse. Desk, two chairs and a sturdy, old-fashioned filing cabinet. There was a cordless phone on a base on the desk, next to a charger for police radios. Pretty dull, even as offices go. Flynn glanced one more time up the stairs before putting his finger to his mouth, saying 'Shush' to the dog, and stepping through the door.

Items of female uniform, including a hat, were hung on a series of hooks on the wall. There was a message log on the desk, a ring binder in which every call-out was recorded by hand, whether it came from a member of the public ringing in directly, calling into the office in person, or a telephone or radio message received from the divisional comms room at Lancaster, the main station covering. Flynn knew it was procedure to log everything. He opened the binder with his fingertip, noticing there were two batteries in the charger, both with the green 'fully charged' lights glowing, and an actual radio next to this. Personal radios were issued to each individual officer now and Flynn assumed this was Cathy's own radio, although it could have been Tom's.

'Mm,' he said at the back of his throat. So wherever she was, he thought, she wasn't in uniform and didn't have her PR with her . . . maybe. Flynn wondered if she and Tom had argued and she had stormed out and was now holed up with a relative or in a hotel somewhere, licking her wounds. It was only speculation, nothing more, Flynn admitted to himself. He could be wrong on all counts. Perhaps Tom simply didn't want to discuss a deeply personal situation. Flynn could empathize with that.

A blank block of message pads was crocodile-clipped to the left side of the message log binder, with several days' worth of messages inserted on to the steel rings on the right-hand side. Flynn started to peek at the top message, which was handwritten – he assumed, by Cathy.

'I thought you were leaving.'

Flynn jerked around to see Tom standing at the office door. He had been able to come silently down the stairs, his approach masked by the sound of the shower. He was still in his dressing gown. 'And you've no right to be in here.'

'Have you two had a fight?' Flynn asked, unperturbed.

'None of your business,' Tom stated.

'Fair do's.' Flynn raised his hands in defeat. 'But I take it you do know where Cathy is?'

Tom pointed towards the front door of the house, saying nothing.

Flynn took the hint and sidled past Tom, who was almost as big as he was. He patted the dog on the way out and as he stepped out into the cold afternoon, the door was slammed behind him. Without a backward glance he walked through the sticking snow to his hire car, spun it around and drove back to the village, stopping outside the pub called the Tawny Owl. A free house, it proclaimed on the sign.

They edged carefully along a tight shale track that clung to the edge of the steep hillside, stumbling occasionally and travelling, according to Henry's compass, slightly north-north-west. Being on the exposed eastern side of the hill, they were completely at the mercy of the weather. The wind had increased forcefully, driving hard sleet-ice remorselessly into their sides as though they were being pelted by gravel.

As much as he was cursing himself for getting them into this mess, Henry was pretty sure they were on the right track. They were just starting the descent down Mallowdale Fell into the valley cut

by the River Raeburn. When they got down to that level, Henry
knew they should be able to find a good track that would lead them
to the civilization that was Kendleton, their stop for the night and
now, of course, the end of their journey. He knew that Donaldson
could not possibly go on, that his friend was in embarrassing and
continual agony. He might even need medical help, although Henry
knew that doctors only dealt with extreme cases of food poisoning
these days. You literally had to excrete it all out of your system, all
by yourself. Probably all that Donaldson needed was TLC, immediate
access to a toilet and a bed to crash on.

Henry stopped. Donaldson had lagged behind. As he waited for
him to catch up, he turned his back to the wind and took out his
mobile phone. Still no signal, but even so he typed out a text message
with a frozen thumb and pressed send, hoping it would wing its
way into the ether anyway. The screen said 'Unable to send message',
so he tried again, pressed the send button, gave a flick of his wrist
as though this would help, and hoped it would somehow land on
Kate's phone.

Donaldson stood miserably behind him. His eyes had sunk into
his face. He looked drawn and exhausted.

'We start going down now.' Henry had to shout above the howling
wind. 'Then there'll be more cover and it should be easier, OK?'
His friend nodded. 'Push on?' Henry asked. Another nod. Henry
turned and started to walk, imagined he heard something – a thud?
– but wasn't certain. Something that wasn't part of the weather
noise. He glanced over his shoulder, expecting to have Donaldson
right behind him.

He wasn't there.

Flynn climbed out of the Peugeot and walked to the front door of
the pub. The snow was now horrendously heavy, falling in a way
he hadn't seen since he'd been a teenager, when winters were much
more severe in this part of the world. It was thick and was definitely
now sticking – almost as soon as he walked through it, leaving
footprints, his tracks were instantly filled in as though he hadn't
been there. He knew at that point that if he was going to get out
of Kendleton that day, now was the time to do it. The weather
looked set and bleak and it wouldn't take long to cut off a village
like this one, set deep in a valley, one road in, one road out.

He decided to do what he needed to do first, then make a

decision about leaving. If he got snowed in, he would just have to throw himself on the mercy of the innkeeper. If necessary he would sleep in the bar, something he'd done on many occasions in the past. The good old days.

He glanced up at the name plate over the door as he went in and saw the licensee's name was displayed as Alison Marsh. He found himself in a very pleasant country pub, low beamed, dark wood, nicely decorated and with a huge fire roaring in a grate. He approached the bar, noticing only a couple of other people in the snug. One was a youngish woman who seemed slightly out of place, sitting alone in an alcove, the other was a grizzled old-timer on a corner seat at the bar who looked as though he'd been rooted there, growing old, for many years. He had a pint of Guinness in front of him, and a whisky chaser. The young woman watched him but the man didn't even raise his eyes from the newspaper he was scanning. Behind the bar was a nice-looking lady, maybe early forties, who smiled at Flynn.

'Hi,' he said, 'Er . . . do you do coffee?'

'You name it.'

'Latte with an extra shot?'

'No problem. Small, medium or large?'

'Medium.'

She nodded and turned to the complex-looking coffee-making contraption at the back of the bar. Flynn eased one cheek of his arse over a bar stool and surveyed the room again. He gave the lone woman a quick smile – she looked away – and the man continued to ignore him.

'Weather not good,' he said to the back of the woman behind the bar.

'No.' The coffee maker gurgled, hissed and steamed. 'It's caught us by surprise and it looks like it could be a bad one.' She turned to him with his foamy drink and placed it carefully on the bar. 'Passing through?'

'Just visiting – but they weren't at home.'

'Ah.' She leaned on the bar and he couldn't help but notice her figure, which was very nice. She caught his look and smiled. 'Two twenty-five, please.'

He paid her, counting out the exact change. When she turned to the till, he pulled a crumpled piece of paper from his pocket and ironed it out on the bar top. Headed 'Lancashire Constabulary

– Message Log', it was a pro-forma document that ensured nothing could be missed when taking a message of any sort from anyone. The top message that Flynn had seen on the pad in Cathy James's office, he had managed to snaffle it in the instant before Tom had appeared at the office door and thrown him out. It was the most recent message she had taken.

Flynn read it, then got out his phone, waited for a few moments for a signal to be indicated on the screen. One didn't. He tutted. He raised his head to the woman behind the bar, who had turned to watch him.

'We struggle out here at the best of times,' she told him. 'They're always on about putting boosters in, or whatever, but they never seem to get round to it. Probably not worth it. This weather will make certain there's no signal at all, I reckon.'

'I take it the landline works?'

'There's a public phone in the toilet corridor.'

Flynn had noticed a phone behind the bar. 'Any chance of using that one?' he asked sweetly. 'Don't want my coffee to go cold.'

She weighed him up, then said, 'OK,' and gave him the cordless handset.

'Thanks. I'm Steve Flynn, by the way.'

'Alison Marsh.'

'Ah, the landlady. Pleased to meet you,' Flynn smiled. He got Cathy James's mobile number from the contacts menu on his own phone and thumbed it into the handset, put it to his ear and waited. A connection was made – then went straight through to voice mail. He tutted and hung up, realizing he was doing a lot of tutting recently.

'No joy?'

'Nah.' He handed the phone back to Alison.

Reading from his stolen message pad, Flynn asked, 'You wouldn't know where Mallowdale House is, would you?'

Flynn saw the woman's instant reaction. 'Why?' she said sharply, and it took him back slightly.

'Is it local?' he asked, carrying on as though nothing had happened.

'Yes.'

'And it's . . . where?'

'Two miles up the road, past the police house.'

'And that's it?'

'Big house, behind a big fence, big grounds.'

'When you say big grounds, what do you mean?'

'Well, the house itself is in big, fenced-in grounds, but the land surrounding that all belongs to Mallowdale.'

'What, like moorland or forest, kind of thing?'

'Yeah – why?'

'Er, nothing,' he said. He picked up his coffee and took a sip. It was a good brew and the extra shot had an instant effect. He was puzzled by Alison's strange reaction as he re-read the message again, written down and recorded by Cathy James, who still remained uncontactable.

In the 'From' section, she had written, '*Anon.*'

In the body of the message she'd written, '*Poachers on Mallowdale House land again.*'

And that was it, very bare bones. Flynn could only imagine the conversation. He guessed the phone must have rung in Cathy's office and she'd answered it: 'Hello, police at Kendleton. PC James speaking. Can I help?' It would have started something like that. Professional, courteous. Then, whoever it was had said, 'There's poachers on Mallowdale House land.' The phone call would have ended abruptly, or she would have quizzed the caller further, asking who was calling, asking for a description of the poacher or poachers, any vehicle, any accompanying animals – such as a dog. But the message was from Mr Anon. It was dated yesterday, timed at 16.30 hours. The words *PC James attending* were scribbled on the bottom of the form.

But Flynn was only guessing. All he had was a sketchy message about poachers from an anonymous source, and no doubt Cathy would have seen it as her duty to investigate, even though yesterday was actually her rest day. What it did was tell Flynn that Cathy had taken a message yesterday afternoon and that Tom was possibly telling lies about having seen her at home. How true was his claim that he hadn't seen her for a couple of days? Or perhaps he wasn't fibbing and they'd just had a big spat that wasn't any business of Flynn's, perhaps everything she'd told Flynn over the phone was just a woman's scorn? Perhaps she was just making things up to get at Tom for something else. What Flynn didn't like, though, was Tom's attitude.

Flynn scratched his head, not really knowing what to think, but he did know that policemen had occasionally come a cropper investigating reports of poachers. He remembered a PC even being murdered. These days poachers weren't jolly characters feeding their families, they were often organized, ruthless gangs and big money was involved, depending on what they were hunting.

He sighed, thinking he should just get the hell out of here before he got trapped.

'I'm curious . . . sorry . . .' Alison interrupted his jagged train of thought. 'Hope you don't mind.'

'About what?'

'Mallowdale House . . . you're not the first person to ask about it today.'

Flynn pouted. 'And?'

'Like I said, I'm curious.' She leaned on the bar again, pushing her breasts tightly against her jumper in a move with obvious consequences for the male of the species, a fact Flynn was certain she was fully aware of.

'To be honest I'd never heard of Mallowdale House until about twenty minutes ago,' Flynn said. His eyes registered the fact that the third finger of her left hand bore no ring of any sort.

'Well, you wanna keep away.'

Flynn blinked. 'You said that without moving your lips,' he said, and he and Alison grinned briefly as both of them turned to the origin of the voice – the old-timer sitting on the stool at the end of the bar, apparently engrossed in his newspaper but actually earwigging. 'What do you mean?'

The man, bearded, dressed in ancient tweeds, raised his chin and said, 'Just an observation, is all.'

Flynn waited for more. Nothing came. He glanced back at Alison and arched his eyebrows.

'They're not that friendly, that's all,' she said, ending the subject.

'Do they have a poaching problem?'

She guffawed. 'Anyone who goes on to Mallowdale land does so at their own risk. The poachers have a problem with the owners, I'd say.'

'Is that a long way of saying no?'

'You work it out.' Clearly the tone of her voice implied that she'd said enough.

Flynn exhaled and thought, 'Bloody villagers.' He was

half-expecting to hear banjos being plucked in the background. 'I see the "No Vacancies" sign is up.'

'Yeah, sorry. I've only got two rooms, both booked for the night. I have actually got six, but the rest are all being renovated and are uninhabitable.'

'Have the guests landed yet?'

'Not so far.'

'Think they will?' He gestured at the weather through the window.

'Why, do you need a room?'

'Considering.'

'I have to give them time to arrive. If they're not here by eight and I haven't heard from them, I'll assume they won't be coming and maybe re-let – if that's any good to you?'

'Sounds half promising.' He threw back the remainder of his coffee and wiped his lips with the paper napkin. 'Nice brew. Maybe see you later.'

Alison leaned on the bar again in the way that stretched her jumper tight. 'Maybe . . . ooh, speak of the devil.' She looked past Flynn's shoulder through the window. 'These are the people who asked about Mallowdale House.'

The blood drained from Flynn's face. Outside, a black Range Rover that Flynn immediately recognized had pulled up in the car park. The one with the impatient driver that had taken off his and another car's wing mirrors. Two men got out. Flynn slid off the bar stool and walked to the door, zipping up his jacket, then stepped back into an alcove as the two men came in through the pub door with a crash and headed to the bar without apparently noticing him.

Flynn noticed Alison's eyes had become wary. The men unzipped their top coats and stomped their feet on the floor to dislodge the snow they'd picked up.

Flynn's mouth went dry as his inner sluice gates opened and adrenalin gushed through his body. In the five years since he'd been a cop, his memory had not dimmed with the passage of time. He recognized that two dangerous men had just entered this out-of-the-way country pub.

Before his departure from the organization he loved, he had spent a good number of years hunting down professional criminals who made their grubby but lucrative living from dealing drugs and causing misery. Not the gofers or the toe-rags on the streets, but those who organized the importation and distribution of the substances had been Flynn's targets. Flynn, as a detective sergeant on the drugs branch with Lancashire Constabulary's Serious and Organized Crime Unit, had successfully targeted some of the leading crime lords in this genre.

Sometimes, of course, he'd been unsuccessful. Often cases built up meticulously over months or years came crashing apart for a variety of reasons.

One such case that he'd been involved in was against a very high-ranking villain called Jonny Cain, maybe one of the richest dealers Flynn had ever encountered. His wealth had been estimated to be somewhere in the region of twenty million. But Cain, a sly, devious man, had eluded the clutches of the law by surrounding himself with layers of protection and operating his business on a cell-by-cell basis. Above all, though, his ruthless approach to anyone who might be a threat to him ensured that few people had the courage to testify against him.

Flynn knew that about a year ago, the police had got Cain as far as a crown court trial for murder, but that had collapsed. Flynn also knew that an unlikely potential witness against Cain – another gangster – had ended up with his brains blown out by a professional assassin. As far as he knew, it had been impossible for the police to prove a definite link between Cain and that killing (although everyone knew it to be the case).

Flynn recalled all this in the moments standing in that alcove because the two men who had just walked into the Tawny Owl, and changed the atmosphere completely, were two of Jonny Cain's most trusted minders.

Flynn had a quick flashback to the Range Rover incident – the slicing off of his door mirror – and bored into his recall of it. Even though the vehicle's windows had been smoked out, he was sure there had been four shapes within and it didn't take a rocket scientist to guess that one of those shapes could well have been Jonny Cain.

Had Cain and the other guy been dropped off at Mallowdale House, Flynn wondered. That was the address that Alison said they'd been enquiring about. And if that was the case, what the hell were they doing here, what did they want and who were they calling on at Mallowdale House?

Flynn dug deep within his mind and regurgitated the names of the two minders: Roy Napier and Sim Riddick, two very evil men who were smiling civilly at Alison. She eyed them cautiously, then glanced in Flynn's direction. The faces of the two men turned the same way and this time they saw Flynn in the alcove, although they gave no sign that they had recognized him.

Quickly he tugged up his collar, gave Alison a quick wave and stepped out into the harsh snowstorm that engulfed the village.

In his right hand was the message about the possible presence of a poacher on Mallowdale House land.

NINE

'Karl! Karl!' Henry bellowed against the heavy snow smashing into his face as he scrambled back up the path. Panic didn't need to rise in him – it was there instantly. He had walked maybe thirty metres along the path from the point at which he and Donaldson had stopped, then, for no reason really, just the hint of the suggestion of an out-of-place noise, he'd looked back to check on the Yank – and he wasn't there. Henry could so easily have walked half a mile with his head down before looking over his shoulder, and if he'd done that and Donaldson hadn't been there . . . That horrendous thought was just one of the many that tumbled though his mind. 'Karl,' he screamed again, reaching the point where they had rested briefly. Henry faced directly into the weather, shouting his friend's name through hands cupped around his mouth.

The path was narrow and precarious. Stepping off it could have serious consequences under any circumstances as the hillside fell sharply away. It was particularly dangerous underfoot because of the steep angle and the loose shale.

It was obvious to Henry what Donaldson had done: taken a step off the path, or simply lost his balance and pitched over the edge.

Henry blasphemed. He had once had food poisoning himself. He recalled it vividly, the whole experience. The creasing gut pain, the shits, the nausea. It had drained him completely of any will power, sucked all the energy out of him. All he had wanted to do was go to bed and curl up like a foetus and pull the sheets over his head and die. At least until the next desperate urge to race to the toilet came. It had also made him woozy and light-headed, and he guessed that could be what had happened to Donaldson.

Henry stood at the edge of what was virtually a precipice, his head shaking as he dithered about what to do. The wind howled around his head and he cocked his ear to one side, trying to listen. He shouted the American's name again.

He was sure he heard some sort of response. The wind swirled away and then there was nothing but the buffeting of the snow, drowning out everything.

Henry shuffled sideways, tentatively placing one foot off the track into the shale. It slid down straight away, but he knew he had to go for it. Angling his whole body to counteract the steepness of the slope he moved down, inches at a time, grinding his feet into the ground with each step.

Within seconds he was enveloped by the snow and had lost sight of the track.

Then he fell and slithered down the hill, emitting a roar, grappling with his fingers, trying to stop his descent. And then he stopped suddenly as he crashed into something hard – which screamed.

'Fuck, Henry,' Donaldson said, as Henry regained his feet and crouched by the curled-up body of his friend.

'What the hell happened? Why did you leave the track?'

'Thought it would be a wheeze,' he gasped. 'A quick way down.'

'You hurt?'

'Yeah – busted my ankle.'

Henry's heart could not have sunk any lower at the words. He crouched over Donaldson with his back to the weather, digging his heels into the shale. Donaldson had managed to sit up.

'Which one?'

'Left.'

'Can you move it?' Henry looked at the left foot as Donaldson tried to rotate it. He grunted as it moved slightly.

'Yep, it moves – but I can feel it swelling in the boot.'

'Hopefully not broken, then?'

'Dunno – feels bad.' He raised his eyes and looked at Henry. 'Pisser, eh?'

Henry nodded. 'Pisser.'

From the directions given, Flynn knew that Mallowdale House was out of the village, beyond the police house, meaning he would have to drive out past Cathy's place again. But he could not bring himself to drive past without speaking to Tom once more. He wasn't remotely happy with what Tom had said to him and he was increasingly concerned about Cathy. He knew she was a big girl, an experienced cop and all that, could look after herself . . . but until he heard from her he wasn't going to be satisfied. His still very active cop instinct told him he needed to dot the i's and cross the t's.

He stopped outside the police station, drumming his fingers on the steering wheel. Decision made, he got out and went up to the front door and pounded it with the side of his fist. Roger the dog responded as before, barking angrily. Flynn kept up the pounding, standing back and checking the windows for any signs of Tom avoiding him. Nothing happened. The dog, from somewhere inside the house, continued to bark.

Flynn then saw there were tyre tracks and footprints in the snow at the garage door, almost filled in again by the snowfall. He walked across to the garage, turned the handle and found it to be unlocked. He pushed open the up-and-over door, which rose easily on its runners and revealed an empty space. Tom's car had gone and the tracks had obviously been made by the vehicle reversing out down the drive. Maybe he had gone to work.

Flynn stepped into the garage and saw there was actually an inner door at the back that led through to the house, into the kitchen. He went to it and heard the snuffling of the dog at the gap along the bottom of the door. Flynn's hand went to the handle, turning it slowly, opening it just a crack and peeking through, seeing the dog's eye.

'Roger,' he cooed softly. 'Roger . . . it's me, Flynnie.' The dog reacted by going frighteningly still. He opened the door another inch. 'Hiya, Roger . . . good lad.' The dog shuffled back a few inches, its eyes watching Flynn intently. Its hackles were up and for an old dog, it looked nasty to Flynn. 'Roger, good lad . . . it's me . . . remember me?'

Roger's ears twitched uncertainly, the beast not knowing what to do – attack or roll over and expose its tummy.

Flynn pushed the door open a little further then extended his hand, not too enticingly he hoped. He saw that it would just about fit into Roger's old jaws very nicely, like a T-bone steak. 'Good lad, come on.' He clicked his tongue. 'That's a boy . . .' Roger blinked, his tail wagged uncertainly, his ears flickering. Flynn opened the door a little further, keeping one hand on the knob, ready to slam it shut if necessary. 'Come on, it's Flynnie . . .'

Then, as if the dog was shedding a raincoat, his whole demeanour changed and he walked forward, head lowered, tail a-wag, ears back, submissive. Flynn was top dog. He patted him on the head, scratched his ears, then took the risk of fully opening the door and stepping into the kitchen. He squatted low, eyes level, and gave Roger a few hearty slaps, watching for any change of mind, but it looked as though Roger was going to do the decent thing – and not rip Flynn's throat out.

'Where's your mum?' Flynn asked. Roger's ears perked up and the big bushy tail wagged enthusiastically. 'Let's find her, shall we?' Flynn stood up and called out Tom's name – just in case. There was no reply. 'Come on,' he said to Roger and walked out of the kitchen, down the hall and into the office.

A quick search did not reveal very much but it did give him some information. A photograph on the wall showed Cathy standing next to a vehicle against the backdrop of the police house. New cop taking up a new beat, Flynn guessed, and the vehicle in question was a short-wheelbase Mitsubishi Shogun, probably the one she used for work and pleasure, part paid for by the county, part paid for by her.

He took out his mobile phone, thinking he would try Cathy's number again, but there was no signal. He picked up the phone on the desk and called it instead, but there was no reply other than the automated response that told him no one was available. He called another number.

'Jerry, old mate . . .' Flynn heard a groan at the other end of the line. 'Sorry to bother you again so soon.'

'You are going to get me sacked,' Jerry Tope said.

'Just a teensy favour.'

'Tch!'

'Knew you'd understand. Just check Cathy James's duty states again, will you?' There was a deep sigh and the tapping of computer keys.

'Rest day, like I said.'

'And Tom James?'

More tapping. 'Nine-five. That it?' Tope asked hopefully.

'Can you get into the computerized incident logs for Kendleton up in Northern Division? Course you can.' Another very pissed-off sigh. 'For yesterday. Can you see if a poacher was reported on land at Mallowdale House?'

Flynn waited. 'Nothing,' Tope said.

'So she didn't call it in, then?' Flynn mused out loud, frowning.

'What?' Jerry asked.

'Nothing – thanks matey.' Flynn was about to hang up when he thought he heard Tope saying something more. 'What was that?'

'I just want to confirm something.'

'What would that be?'

'Are you talking about Mallowdale House in Kendleton?'

'Yes.'

'I assume you know who lives there?'

'Unfriendly people, I gather. Lord of the manor, I suppose. Shoots commoners just as soon as look at them.'

'Not quite. An OC target,' Tope said. 'A very big OC target.'

'Organized crime as in . . .?'

'You didn't hear this from me.'

'Just tell me.'

'Jack Vincent.'

Flynn's brain cogs whirred. 'No bells,' he admitted.

'Rich, connected, usually operates down below the radar, business fronts mainly in haulage and construction.'

'Drugs?'

'Big style. Came into our sights say three years ago.'

'Which is why I don't know him.'

'And that's all I'm saying – especially on an open line.'

'I happen to be sitting in Cathy James's office, using her phone, buddy.'

'Why the hell are you asking me what shift she's working, then?'

'Because she isn't here. I broke in.' Flynn hung up quickly, smiling at the wind-up. Then he leaned forward and looked at the message logs, as he thought this through. He knew it wouldn't be unusual for a deployment at a rural station not to be logged immediately with the control room, although eventually it would be; nor was it unusual for a rural beat officer to turn out on a rest day. That was the downside that came with working a rural beat, you were at the behest of the community 24/7 and rest days were a luxury. Having said that, Flynn would have expected Cathy to inform control room that she was attending the report of a poacher, if only from a health and safety perspective. He frowned, flicked idly through a few days' worth of messages, some handwritten, others word processed, and realized with shock that he'd made a very big assumption about something. He took out the now very crumpled message he'd stolen earlier that day from the top of the pad, straightened it out and re-read it.

Somehow they managed to make it back up the steep hillside to the track, Henry taking Donaldson's weight and half lifting, half dragging him. By the time they were back on the narrow track, Henry was seriously exhausted. He settled the big man down and re-checked the mobile phones, shaking his head angrily, again resisting the compulsion to fling the useless items into the snow when they showed no signal.

'I reckon we've got about two miles to go, max, before we hit the village. By my estimation we should be pretty close to an unused quarry which we'll skirt around and from there we should be able to find a decent road down to the main road, then we'll be near the village.'

'Is this good news?'

'It's all good news. How's the foot, ankle, whatever?'

'I don't think it's broken, but it's a bad sprain.'

'So it might as well be broken?'

Donaldson shrugged helplessly. 'Guess so.'

'We'll do it bit by bit, yard by yard, eh?' He patted Donaldson's shoulder, dreading how hard this was going to be. Henry was big and strong enough, but Donaldson was bigger and heavier and the prospect of keeping him upright for the next two miles across treacherous terrain and against the weather did not fill Henry with glee. The drag back up the hill, only a matter of fifty metres, had been tough enough. 'All I ask is that you don't go on any unauthorized excursions again,' Henry said.

'Are we going to find your mummy?' Flynn asked the dog in his most patronizing tone. 'Yes we are, yes we are.' Roger barked happily. 'Are you going to come with me? For a walk?' Roger's ears shot up at the 'W' word and Flynn could have sworn he smiled and went, 'Yeah, yeah.'

Flynn had a quick scout around the kitchen and found a selection of leads hanging behind the back door, chunky thick leather ones, ones that looked like chains from a work gang, and an extendable one. Flynn picked a leather one, clipped it to Roger's collar and looped the handle a couple of times around his hand to keep a firm hold of him, otherwise the dog would probably do just what it wanted to do. Before leaving, Flynn cast his eyes around the room and saw a lady's headscarf tossed across a kitchen stool. Assuming it was Cathy's, he grabbed it and stuffed it in his pocket.

'Come on then, Roger.' Even before he had completed the sentence the dog lunged for the door, almost yanking Flynn's shoulder out of its socket. He heaved back. 'Whoa there.'

It had some effect, but Flynn was still basically dragged out of the door, into the garage and out to the front of the house where the dog made a beeline for a big tree at the bottom of the drive and cocked his leg up. After the relief, Flynn took better command and led the dog to his hire car, opened the passenger door and indicated for Roger to climb in. After a suspicious glance, the dog climbed stiffly in and Flynn noticed for the first time that its back legs were on their way out, as is often the case with German shepherds, or so he had heard.

Flynn went to the driver's side, got in. Roger was almost as large as a human passenger and Flynn felt like he was sitting next to Scooby-Doo, the cartoon dog.

'Ready?'

Roger eyed him, his tongue hanging out, slavering all over the gear lever.

Donaldson did his utmost to help Henry, but it was clear that the pain of the ankle injury and the continuing griping in the stomach from the food poisoning had combined to knock him for six. Henry had Donaldson's arm across his shoulder, acting as a crutch for his friend, but the going underfoot was slippery and the track hardly wide enough for two to walk abreast. But Henry held on and they made slow progress. The weather did not let up and daylight was fading fast.

Henry had no reason to suspect his estimation of their position was anything other than correct, but they still had to get down off the hill and into the village before nightfall. To be caught even a hundred yards away from the main road would be just as deadly as being trapped on the hill.

Steve Flynn drove up the narrow road. It was filling with snow, which was starting to drift and bank up in various places. He cursed the weather and had another quick flashback to the sunshine he'd abandoned two thousand miles south of here.

With the weather being so bad, he realized he didn't have time for more than a cursory drive around the roads that formed the perimeter of some of the land surrounding Mallowdale House. It didn't help that he was a stranger to the area, didn't know where he was going, didn't know what he was looking for and was probably wasting his time anyway.

The road dipped, the car fishtailed through some deep snow, then began to rise. On his left was a high security fence and he spotted a sign written in red letters which he guessed warned against trespassing. On a post behind one of the signs, behind the fence, he also saw a CCTV camera. He didn't stop to read the signs, but drove on another hundred metres and found a wide double gate, maybe ten feet high, but dipping slightly in the centre where the two halves met. He pulled up at it, peered through the windscreen and considered it for a moment. It seemed to be the entrance to Mallowdale House.

'You stay here,' he told Roger, who nodded.

He got out and walked up to the gate, which was made of solid wood, reinforced with steel belts, and was electronically operated. On a pole behind one of the gate posts was another CCTV camera, focused on him. There was another sign on the gate itself which read, its tone unfriendly, 'MALLOWDALE HOUSE. NO TRESPASSING. GROUNDS PATROLLED BY SECURITY GUARDS AND DOGS. BEWARE. KEEP AWAY. CCTV CAMERAS ALSO IN USE.' Like the sign further down the road, it was written in red. He tried to peer through the tiny gap in the middle of the gate. With one eye he could just about see a curved driveway, with a couple of sets of tyre tracks in the snow, and beyond, behind the snow-laden trees, almost out of sight, a large house, but he couldn't make out its detail in the fading light. He could also make out some cars parked outside, but again, no detail.

'Can I help you?' Flynn jumped as a metallic voice came from an intercom speaker set in the gate post. Automatically he glanced at the CCTV camera again. He gave a little wave, walked over to the intercom and pressed the talk button.

'I'd like to see Mr Vincent,' Flynn said, off the cuff.

'What's your business?'

Still winging it, Flynn ad-libbed, 'Police business. I believe he's had poachers on his land.'

'Show your warrant card to the camera,' the voice instructed him.

Flynn made a weedy show of patting his pockets. 'I think I've forgotten it.'

'In that case, come back when you've got it – and make an appointment beforehand.' The intercom clicked dead.

Flynn toyed with the idea of pressing the talk button again, but decided against it. He got back in the car and looked at his travelling companion. 'Have you got your warrant card?' he asked the dog. Roger looked dumbly at him, dipped his head forward to be stroked and dribbled on to Flynn's lap. 'Thought not.'

He engaged first gear and carefully started the car, the wheels spinning in the snow. He drove on up the hill. The high fencing with warning signs continued for another quarter of a mile parallel with the road before doing a right-hand turn. Flynn drove on up the hillside, which got steeper and steeper, passing the entrance to Mallowdale Quarry. He wondered if this had any connection with the house, recalling what Jerry Tope had said about Jack Vincent's legitimate businesses, haulage and construction. The light car became even more difficult to control and the snow seemed to be getting even heavier the higher up he got.

Flynn realized he was driving blind in more senses than one and he might simply be reacting to something that didn't even exist. Chances were that Cathy was completely safe and unharmed. She'd probably stormed out of the house with no intention of looking for a poacher and was safe and sound somewhere, licking her wounds, phone turned off to stop incoming calls from Tom. Flynn still felt uneasy about the situation and was worried that Cathy wasn't returning his calls, but he could see there was very little he could do about it and a big part of his instinct was telling him not to get involved. Domestic disputes equalled messy nightmares.

He decided to give it another mile or so then – literally, probably – spin around, slide back down to the village and see how the weather panned out.

The road twisted. The car slid and the steering wheel spun out of his grip, and he almost ended up nose first in a snow bank.

'Enough's enough, yeah?' he asked Roger, who had only just managed to stay seated. Flynn reversed carefully, keeping the revs low and using the clutch tenderly to edge back off the road into a forest track. His intention was to return to Kendleton and, if there was no chance of leaving the village because of the weather, throw his charming self on the mercy of Alison the curvy landlady for the night. He tried not to think about the possibility of laying his weary head on her bosom . . . the car slithered backwards on to the track, making him concentrate on driving again. He braked, went back into first gear and let out the clutch slowly. The tyres spun, not gripping. He eased off and tried again.

It was then he happened to glance in the rear view mirror. Something dark amongst the pine trees had caught his eye. Puzzled, not even sure if he had seen anything, he yanked on the handbrake and looked over his shoulder through the back window, which was covered with big spats of snow. It cleared with a sweep of the wiper blade and confirmed the glimpse. There was a dark vehicle parked some thirty metres up the track, virtually out of sight of the road.

Flynn's guts felt as though they'd been scraped out as he fumbled with his seat belt, scrambled out of the car and ran up the track.

They staggered towards the remains of a farmhouse, nothing more than a shell of stone and rubble, no roof, most of the walls missing. It looked as though it had been bombed, but it was a good sight for Henry to behold. Breathing heavily, he was close to falling over. Cold pervaded his whole being and his energy reserves had dwindled almost to zero as he fought to keep Donaldson upright, as he had been doing for the last two tortuous miles.

He was relieved to see the building because it was a feature on his map, overlooking the edge of the disused quarry which was also on the map. This meant they were not far from a track that would lead them down to the minor road, thence to the village of Kendleton where they could rest and recuperate and possibly get medical attention. The end was in sight.

He guided Donaldson to the farmhouse and eased him down under the lee of one of the walls that remained standing, blocking off some of the wind and snow.

Henry's relief was incredible, but tempered by the thought he might have made a mistake in stopping. Should they have carried on? The thought of heaving his friend back up to his feet was demoralizing. Henry stretched his back, muscles he didn't know he had ached agonizingly. He looked at Donaldson massaging his injured ankle. His tanned face was pale and sickly.

'Couple of minutes, then we get going again.'

'Sure thing,' Donaldson mumbled, not even raising his eyes to look at Henry.

Henry resisted the urge to sink down next to him, knowing he would not want to get back up again and also wanting to give his friend the impression that he was OK, even if he wasn't. A psychological thing, his desire to keep Donaldson's spirits up.

Instead he wandered around the building that had once been a large farmhouse, curious as to why it had never been renovated. To Henry it looked like it would have made a stunning house. He wandered around the walls then got the probable answer to the question. Within ten feet of the gable end was a high, wire-mesh fence. Henry walked towards it, slipped his fingers through the mesh and gave it a rattle, reading the *Danger – Keep Out* sign in red. Underneath these words was written *Disused Quarry*. And that was why the farmhouse had never been done up, he guessed. Too near the rim of the quarry, although as he peered through the fence he couldn't actually see this. But he assumed it wasn't too far away. Once, the farmhouse would have been situated in a stunning location on the hillside, but as the quarry had been excavated and crept closer, it wasn't so nice.

'Whatever,' Henry said, ending his speculation. He turned, had his back to the fence when suddenly the hairs on the back of his neck rose and a very strange sensation rippled down his spine as he became aware of a presence behind him. For a brief moment every organ in his body seemed to seize as the certainty overwhelmed him that somewhere behind him, not too far away, something was stalking him.

He went rigid. Out of the corner of his eye he was utterly convinced he had seen a movement, a shape on the other side of the fence. His mouth opened slightly and he swallowed. Something deep inside him, some long-buried intuition, told him he was being hunted, that he was the prey.

Catching his breath, his neck muscles taut like wire, his nostrils flaring, his mouth now a tight 'O', he spun quickly. Was there something? An indistinguishable shape on the other side of the fence? Yes. Then it was gone and there was just the faintest scent in the air. Henry stared dumbly at the fence, at the exact point where he was certain he'd seen something. But there was nothing and he became conscious of how wound up his body had become.

Relief wafted over him and he laughed with embarrassment.

'A deer,' he thought. Couldn't have been anything else. Might not even have been a deer – just nothing, a combination of tiredness and over-imagination and light-headedness. Maybe the equivalent of the thirsty desert traveller seeing an oasis, then realizing it was a mirage, pure hallucination.

He shook his head, exhaled, relaxed himself and returned to his friend. This time Donaldson lifted his face weakly when Henry stood in front of him.

'Not far to go, pal,' Henry said, proffering his hand. Donaldson reached out pathetically and Henry tried to ease him up. The big man rose slowly, painfully and almost got to his feet, then seemed to stagger and lose balance as he put weight inadvertently on his injured ankle. Henry's hands shot out to steady him, but Donaldson moaned and slid back down on to his backside, dragging Henry with him.

'Jeez, sorry pal. It just went.'

'It's OK,' Henry reassured him. 'Let's do it slow and sure.' Henry positioned himself on his haunches, slightly to one side of Donaldson, and took hold of his left arm with both hands, but when he looked up he was staring into the golden eyes of a beast.

TEN

Flynn jogged through the snow, slowed and eventually walked the remaining few yards to the vehicle, a black, short-wheelbase Mitsubishi Shogun: Cathy's car. The one Flynn had seen in the photograph in the office, the one she was proudly standing against with the police house in the background. About two inches of snow had settled on the roof and bonnet.

It was parked on the track in the trees and as Flynn glanced around and back he confirmed it was just out of sight of the road, being parked on a slight right-hand kink in the track. It would be virtually impossible for anyone driving past to have spotted it, and even if it had been seen, so what? Nothing that suspicious.

Other than the fact it belonged to the local bobby, who hadn't been seen or heard of for a day . . . but again, who would know that?

Flynn's horrible gut feeling started to become even more painful.

He peered in through the side windows, wiping the snow off with the blade of his right hand, shading his eyes to see inside. The vehicle was empty. He tried the driver's door, found it unlocked. He pulled it open and leaned inside, looking over into the back seat, seeing nothing of interest. However, on the front passenger seat was a sturdy leather handbag of the type issued to female officers. Flynn dragged it across to him, opened it and peered at the contents. A pink duty diary, a couple of bits and pieces of make-up, a CS spray canister, an extendable baton, a pair of rigid handcuffs and a mobile phone.

'Not happy,' he said, 'not happy.' He was tempted to handle the items but held back for the time being, because he thought this could well be part of a crime scene and he didn't want to contaminate any possible evidence with his fingerprints. Again he considered he was maybe being over-dramatic. But, he thought, recalling good police practice, it was better than having egg chucked in your face. You can laugh off making an arse of yourself, but you can never shrug off overlooking something of importance.

He just didn't like it – at all.

Then he noticed the key was still slotted into the ignition. He extracted it carefully, closed the door and locked the car with the remote. He quickly ran his hand under the thick blanket of snow on the bonnet and confirmed to himself that the engine really was cold. Then he walked back to his hire car and looked in at Roger, still sitting patiently. Well trained, these county dogs, he thought.

Flynn opened the door, muttering to the dog, 'You're not going to like this, pal.' He attached the extending lead and hooked it on to Roger's collar. The dog clambered stiffly out and dashed to the nearest tree to cock his leg up. Flynn waited for the flow to end, then said, 'C'mon Roger, where's your mum? Come on, find your mum.' He pulled out the scarf he'd taken from the kitchen and let the dog sniff it.

Roger's ears perked up and he lunged excitedly up the track with a woof, almost dislocating Flynn's shoulder from its socket, and headed towards the Shogun. Flynn tried to rein him back to get more control. To some degree he was successful, but Roger certainly had a mind of his own and obviously knew his job, so Flynn let the lead reel out a little.

At the car, the dog sniffed around, encouraged by Flynn's words. He rose up on his back legs and placed his massive front paws on the driver's door window, making Flynn appreciate just what a huge dog he was, more like a fully grown man in a dog suit. He shoved his wet nose to the glass and slavered on it, then pushed himself away from the vehicle and dragged Flynn up the track, zigzagging as he went, nose-down in the snow, foraging, pausing occasionally to sniff the air, or a particularly interesting tree trunk.

Flynn sensed the dog was on to something. At least up to the point where he stopped, sniffed and pawed the ground. Flynn approached with trepidation, drawing the lead back on to the inertia reel, thinking that something – someone – had been found in a shallow grave. His imagination ran riot.

The dog circled tightly, dropped his back end and started to shit.

Flynn didn't know whether to be relieved or annoyed, but the expression of pure pleasure on Roger's face actually made him chuckle. Then, with one last squeeze, Roger had completed his task and was ready to resume the search. He went up the track, pulling Flynn behind him. Flynn remarked philosophically, 'When you gotta go, you gotta go.'

For an old dog with arthritic joints, Roger moved quickly and with purpose. It was all Flynn could do to keep up and prevent the lead from wrapping around trees and snagging bushes. Flynn knew that police dog handlers usually allowed their dogs to roam freely on wide searches, but he didn't want to face the prospect of never seeing Roger again and having to explain that away.

The ground was broken and uneven underneath the snow and it was hard to keep upright, but Flynn was fit and agile and controlling Roger reminded him, in a way, of playing a marlin. Not as much fun, obviously. The path rose steeply and Flynn saw they were making their way up alongside a high fence on their right. Suddenly they reached a plateau which opened up at a dilapidated farm building.

Then it was as though Roger had an injection of speed. He surged ahead, uttering a growl, and hurtled towards the building. The lead played out like a fishing line from a spool. The dog skittered and half-disappeared behind a wall that had once been one of the gable-ends of the old farmhouse.

Flynn rushed up behind him as Roger stopped abruptly and dropped into a rigid attacking stance, hackles rising, ears flattened back, a very dangerous snarl, revealing thick, long, sharp canines. His teeth were stained brown with age, but even so they looked like they could still tear off a man's biceps when combined with the powerful muscles in the jaw.

Flynn skidded around the corner, the inertia reel clattering like a broken tape measure as it gathered back the lead. He almost collided with Roger, whose training had taken over as he stood looking ferociously at the two bedraggled, exhausted and weather-beaten men he had discovered sheltering in the protection provided by the crumbling wall.

Roger glanced at Flynn, waiting for the attack signal. Flynn let the lead rattle all the way back in until it was as short as it could be, then he thumbed on the locking mechanism. Only then did he look properly at the men.

The one who'd been on his haunches, almost eye-to-eye with Roger, rose unsteadily, knees cracking. The other one, sitting against the wall, stayed where he was.

'Bloody hell,' Flynn gasped. 'Henry-freaking-Christie. What are you doing here?'

'I could ask you the same question,' Henry croaked.

'Walking my dog, obviously,' Flynn said.

'I never thought I'd be glad to see you,' Henry admitted. 'Need some help here.'

As they helped Donaldson to his feet, Flynn inadvertently knocked the locking catch on the lead and Roger, now uninterested in his find, moseyed off towards the fence. Flynn kept hold of the lead, but did not watch what he was doing.

Roger raised his sensitive nose and sniffed the air. A change came over him: his head fell and his hackles rose again as they had done on finding the two men, but this time he stepped backwards, his throat rumbling uncertainly. There was a terrible growl from the other side of the fence. Roger leapt a foot high, all four paws leaving the ground, turned tail and ran back to Flynn, coming around him and wrapping the lead around his legs, taking cover.

Henry and Flynn looked from the dog to the fence and back again.

'What the hell was that?' Flynn said, stepping out of the lasso

formed by the lead and hunching one of Donaldson's arms around
his shoulders.

'Don't know – an owl?' Henry suggested.

'Big owl,' Flynn said.

They manhandled the sick and lame Donaldson between them the
mile or so back down the hill, passing the Shogun on the way, and
eased him on to the back seat of Flynn's hired Peugeot where he
slumped gratefully across the upholstery with a groan. Flynn
switched on the engine and turned up the fan heater a few notches.

'It's not far to the village from here,' Flynn said, blowing into
his cupped hands. Darkness was almost upon them, the snow unre-
lenting. 'This could cut the place off,' he said, gesturing at the
weather. 'We probably need to get going, otherwise the road from
here could be impassable, too.'

'Yeah, good idea,' Henry agreed. 'Shall we?' He indicated the car.

'But not just yet,' Flynn said.

'He needs to get somewhere warm,' Henry said.

'And I reckon I've got another ten minutes of looking,' Flynn
said.

Henry regarded him. His face felt frozen and unfeeling, his fingers
inside his gloves like ice-pops, and all he wanted to do was defrost.
'Just what the hell are you doing here?' he asked. 'What are you
looking for? I'm here because an ill-judged jaunt went wrong, but
you're two thousand miles off your patch, aren't you?' If he was
honest, he did not care what Flynn was up to or why, he was simply
grateful their paths had collided, thankful for his assistance with
Donaldson, and now he just wanted a hot bath, hot food and to get
his friend sorted. He had no interest in Flynn's circumstances.

'I couldn't resist a plea from a husky maiden,' Flynn said, not
giving Henry the additional reasons he'd left Gran Canaria, such as
the possibility of an assault complaint, or the lack of work. 'So I've
turned up here and, to cut a long story short, I think I'm looking
for a body.' He pointed to the Shogun up the track. 'That's her car.
Her keys and possessions were in it, but she's nowhere to be found.
I'm thinking bad things.'

'And who is the dusky maiden?' Henry said, playing along with
reluctance.

'Cathy James, the rural beat officer out here.'

Henry would have frowned, but the cold had made his forehead as smooth and fixed as if he'd had a Botox injection. 'A police officer?'

'You might remember her as Cathy Turnbull – if you know her at all.'

Henry's internal light bulb flickered. 'She married Tom James, a detective from Lancaster.'

'The very one.'

'He's a good lad,' Henry said. Flynn emitted a doubtful noise. Henry relented a little and tried to show some interest. 'So what's going on?'

'Nutshell? I got a few frantic calls from Cathy – we go way back,' he explained. 'I turned up here and found she hasn't been seen since a domestic ding-dong. Good lad Tom acts like he doesn't give a shit and now I've found her car.' He opened his arms helplessly.

'Where does the dog come into it?'

Flynn gave Henry a pissed-off look. 'Does it matter? Fact is, I can't contact her, I've found her car in the middle of nowhere and I'm worried – as you would be,' he concluded cynically.

'But no sign of any body?' Henry asked.

'No . . . but I also know she might've been checking up on a report of a poacher on this land, so that's an add-on worry. I mean, she could've come a cropper challenging a poacher, dunno. It's happened before, hasn't it? And as for the dog, it's hers, so I borrowed him to look for her.'

Flynn was not one of Henry's favourite people, and their history was one of conflict. However, as a cop, he felt some responsibility to act on Flynn's story, half-baked as it was. He looked up at the sky, then at the Peugeot with Donaldson in the back seat. If he insisted on getting Donaldson to the village, there would be no light left at all, and as there was only a few minutes' worth left anyway, he decided that he would humour Flynn. At least then he couldn't be criticized. 'Let's have a look at the car, then.'

'What about your mate?'

'A few more minutes won't do him any harm. It'll be pitch black then anyway and there won't be any time to look for anything.'

Flynn gave a short, grateful nod. He tugged Roger's lead and the three of them walked back up to Cathy's Shogun. Flynn took the opportunity to give Henry a few more details of what had been going on. Henry listened as he trudged. Flynn pointed the remote at the car and unlocked it as they got to it, the inner light coming on. Henry opened the driver's door, leaned carefully in, checking the interior. He picked up the leather handbag Flynn had told him about and peered at the contents, glancing sideways at Flynn.

'Admittedly, looks sus,' Henry conceded. 'If she was getting out to deal with a poacher, why would she leave this stuff behind?'

'Maybe she didn't get the chance,' Flynn said.

Henry jerked his head in acknowledgement, and thought, *Or maybe she didn't feel the need to have the stuff with her, or maybe this is just the set-up of a hysterical person trying to draw attention to herself.* He kept those musings to himself.

'Did she actually say what the problem was with her and Tom?' Henry asked.

'Not really,' Flynn said in a strained way. 'But she did say something weird.'

Henry waited.

'She said her husband was bent.'

'As in gay, or cop?'

'Cop.'

'Mm, I find that hard to believe, knowing what I do of Tom James.'

'You didn't seem to find it hard to believe when you were investigating me,' Flynn blurted, displaying deep-rooted resentment.

Henry blinked. 'A million quid did go missing,' he pointed out.

'And I didn't take it, as I've since proved.'

'Let's not go there.' Henry raised his eyebrows.

Flynn pursed his lips and said, 'Whatever.'

Henry reached back inside the Shogun and lugged out a big Maglite torch from the passenger footwell. 'Let's give it a once round the vehicle, say a ten-metre circle, the vehicle being the centre. I reckon we take a quick look and if we find nothing, we come back in the morning.'

Sullenly, Flynn nodded, unable to believe his own little outburst, still surprised at how much his past dealings with Henry still rankled with him. Scratch the surface, he thought bitterly, you uncover a cancer.

'You want to try the dog again?'

'On the whole, I think he might have lost the knack,' Flynn admitted sadly, patting Roger's head.

Henry switched on the torch. The strong beam cut through the gloom, the snow looking eerie as it fell through the light. He walked to the front of the car and tried to fix his mind on the situation. It didn't help that all he wanted was to get off the damned hillside, not go scratting around in the undergrowth. Every bit of him was cold. His feet were sopping wet now, his gloves had been penetrated by the damp and although his outer clothing had done its job well, he was chilled to the marrow and fed up with it.

Truth was, he didn't want to do this. His instinct was to remove Cathy's property from the car, lock the vehicle up and leave it in situ overnight; get back to civilization, then start from scratch in the morning. What he was doing now was just a sop to appease Flynn, someone he didn't like very much and who was developing a nasty habit of coming back into his life to haunt him.

'I'll have a look over there,' he said, no enthusiasm in his voice.

'Don't try too hard,' Flynn said, responding to Henry's tone.

Henry set off from the front radiator grille of the Shogun. He intended to walk ten yards dead ahead, five yards to the left, left again, then back to the car, kicking up snow and dirt as he went. His feeling was that if Cathy had come to grief, and this wasn't an elaborate ploy to get attention, the grief would have happened in fairly close proximity to the car. Not that her body couldn't have been dragged further into the trees after the deed had been done.

As he walked forward, he wondered why he hadn't switched on the car headlights. Brain freeze, he thought. Knackered. No time for this shit. Want to go home.

The snow got deeper the further he walked from the car. He glanced over his shoulder and saw the shadowy figure of Flynn covering the area on the nearside of the car, accompanied by what looked in the dark like a wolf.

It didn't matter that he wasn't looking where he was going because he would probably have caught his foot and stumbled on the snow-covered root anyway. He kicked the obstruction angrily, but it wasn't quite solid enough to be part of a tree, because it moved. Curious, he poked at it again with his toe and unearthed a frozen arm. He dropped to one knee, brushed away the snow until he revealed the white, frozen face of a dead woman.

'Over here,' he said, then louder, 'Steve, over here.'

ELEVEN

Flynn stared incredulously at Henry. They were standing either side of the body in the snow and Flynn could not quite believe the words that had just spilled from Henry's cold-hearted mouth.

'Let me put this in simple terms,' Flynn's voice rose angrily. 'I owe you at least one good punch in the mouth for the way you stitched me up way back when, and I'm damn sure I can get away with it out here. So, if you do what I think you want to do, I won't hang back.' He paused. 'No way on earth is this body going to stay out here.'

Henry allowed Flynn his little rant and could not resist saying, 'And when I hear shit like that coming out of your mouth, I realize Lancashire Constabulary is a much better organization without people like you in it.'

Flynn bridled like a prodded Rottweiler.

Henry went on quickly, sensing Flynn's inner burning. 'All I'm saying is that if we start messing around here and moving the body, we're likely to lose evidence. You don't get a second chance . . .'

'At a crime scene,' Flynn completed the sentence sourly for him, quoting the Murder Investigation Manual. 'I know all that, but by implication you are actually suggesting that somehow her body should be left here until you can get the circus out to it. That could be . . . fuck knows when!'

'I'm simply considering all the angles, pros and cons.' Henry had to raise his voice against an ever strengthening wind. He jabbed his finger downwards at the body between them, already re-covered in snow after Henry had brushed some of it away only moments before. 'She's been murdered and I don't want to lose any evidence that might help catch a killer. Especially as she's a colleague.'

'And that would mean leaving her here?' Flynn demanded.

'In an ideal world, yes. If the weather was fine and we could actually communicate with someone and I could get the circus out and I could protect it and leave it guarded – that's exactly what I'd do.'

'But none of those things apply.'

'I know – but what I need to do is find out the true situation, OK? Our mobiles don't seem to work out here, but are we actually cut off by road yet? Until I get to a landline and put a call through to headquarters I won't know for certain. Can I get a helicopter up? Can I get a team here? Until I get those questions answered I won't make a decision.' Henry's jaw jutted challengingly.

Flynn relented slightly. 'Tell you what, you go to the village, use my motor, and see if you can contact your precious HQ and find out what the score is. I'll lay odds nothing's moving, not in this neck of the woods anyway. I'll stay and cover the scene – if you'll allow me to sit in the Shogun.'

And then there was the other aspect: Henry was also suspicious of Flynn, as he would be of anyone so closely connected to a murder victim. Did he do it?

As if Flynn could read Henry's mind, he said, 'No – I didn't.'

They weighed each other up for a few moments, then Henry nodded and said, 'Start the car to keep warm, but don't touch anything.'

'I was a cop for twenty years,' Flynn said. 'I know what to do.' Henry handed him the torch. 'And if you can't get anyone out, this body is being moved, whatever the hell you say or want.'

Unfazed by Flynn, Henry said, 'I'll be making the decisions.'

Flynn watched Henry stumble back past the Shogun to the hire car, shaking his head at the detective's back, somehow stopping himself from jerking a middle finger up at his back. Then he looked down at the body at his feet, squatted down and shone the torch beam on to her distorted face, or at least what was left of it. The top right-hand quadrant had been effectively blown off, undoubtedly from a shotgun blast at close range. The right eye had also been removed, but even though the force of the blast had caused the remaining three-quarters to be hideously misshapen, the lips baring the teeth, the cheek distended, Flynn could still clearly recognize Cathy James.

'Oh babe,' he whispered, trying to hold back his anguish, 'who the hell did this to you?' But even as he asked a dead body, Flynn was pretty positive that the husband had some very difficult questions to answer.

Henry dropped heavily into Flynn's hire car and dragged the seat belt cross his chest.

'What's happening?' Donaldson's weak voice came from the rear. He was lying in a foetal position across the back seat, knees brought up tightly to his chest.

'Tell you later. I'm going to get you down to the pub, then I need to get back up here.'

'You found a body or something?'

'Something like that.'

'Oh,' he said with little interest, showing how poorly he was.

Thick snow covered the windscreen, heavy and wet. The wipers had to work hard to clear the glass before Henry put the car into first and slowly eased out the clutch.

'How're you feeling?' he asked. The car crept forward, off the forest track, on to the road. He turned left into the gradient and instantly the front wheels failed to grip. The car slewed in slow motion across the snow. Henry wrestled with the wheel, turned into the skid and corrected it. He realized that although there was only a couple of miles or so to go, it was going to have to be a slow journey.

'Jeepers,' Donaldson said, grabbing the back of Henry's seat to stop himself pitching off his own seat into the footwell.

'Sorry,' Henry said.

'And in answer to your question, not good. Ankle's throbbing like it's on a hotplate and the insides are still churning. Should I elaborate?'

'No.' Henry leaned forward as he drove, his chin almost on the rim of the steering wheel, nose nearly touching the screen as though this position made it easier to see ahead and control the car.

'Who was that guy anyway? Why – how – do you know him?'

'Ex-cop,' Henry said. 'I gave him a helping hand in the ex department.'

'Ahh.' Donaldson's stomach cramped tightly. 'Need a restroom,' he said, and added, 'pretty urgently.'

'I'm going as fast as I can,' Henry said, trying to concentrate on the road and not put the car into a ditch. Going at this snail's pace required all his skill and focus, even though several other things were tumbling simultaneously through his mind, mainly the dead body of a cop and the presence of Steve Flynn, with whom he had crossed swords five years earlier and who had reappeared the previous year in connection with a case Henry had been investigating – a case that had links with the reason Flynn had left the police.

In respect of the body – the important thing – Henry knew the scene had to be protected, hence his quandary about how to proceed for the best. Despite being en route to check it out, he was as sure as Flynn that because of the atrocious weather, there would be no chance of turning anyone out to assist him. His call to HQ would serve no purpose other than to alert the powers that be that a colleague had been murdered and a team had to be on standby, ready to deploy as soon as the weather allowed. He really wanted to leave the body in situ, and the evidence-gathering part of him was convinced this was the sensible thing to do, for the reason he'd lectured Flynn: no second chance at a crime scene.

But Henry knew this was unlikely to be an option, either practically – who would guard the scene on the worst night of the year? – or from a humanitarian point of view. And because of the weather, evidence would be destroyed anyway. Based on that, Henry knew that, somehow, he had to recover the body and try to maintain the integrity of the scene at the same time.

As he corralled the car down the hill, Henry was suddenly confronted by the appearance of a black Range Rover coming up in the opposite direction, headlights blazing on full beam. Henry squinted and flashed his own lights, but the big car continued to hog two-thirds of the road and forced the smaller car on to the grass verge. Henry just managed to keep control.

He cursed, flicked the wheel this way and that, and the two cars passed within centimetres of each other. He added a few more colourful phrases, but the incident passed without anyone dying, so Henry stuffed it out of his mind and continued on, very bloody annoyed by everything: the adventure – two mates on a well-deserved walking break – had gone boobs-up and now he had to put on his Senior Investigating Officer cap when all he wanted to do was chill out and recover. He knew that this day was far from over.

Passing the snow-covered sign declaring he was entering the village of Kendleton – safe drivers welcome – he kept his eyes on scan, taking in a few things of interest that might be of assistance to him in the coming hours, such as a tractor parked on the main road, before slithering to a stop outside the Tawny Owl. The old pub was a welcoming sight, promising warmth and comfort.

'Let's get you into your room,' he said over his shoulder to Donaldson, who was emitting weak, pathetic noises as he clung on desperately to prevent a bowel movement. 'Toilet first, though,' Henry corrected himself.

He helped him out, in through the front door, and propelled him gently along in the direction of the loo before turning to the bar.

There were only a handful of customers, unsurprisingly considering the weather. Henry approached the bar, his finger-ends tingling as he took off his gloves, and the warmth of the roaring fire immediately caressed him. He peeled off his outer jacket, fighting the urge to order a double scotch and sink into the battered, empty armchair by the fireplace. The last thing he wanted to do was turn out again, but relaxation and recovery were distant concepts at the moment, and were soon to get further away.

The lady behind the bar turned away from the two men she'd been serving at the far end and came towards Henry. Even in his tired state he could not fail to appreciate her looks and figure and, as if by years of conditioning, he tilted his head slightly and gave her his boyish grin. On a man his age, it probably came across as more of a leer.

'What can I get you?'

'My friend and I have two rooms booked for tonight,' he said. Instantly the expression on her face changed to one of horror.

'Ahh,' she said, drawing out the word.

'Under the name of Christie,' he added helpfully.

'Mm, yes . . . unfortunately I've had to let the rooms to someone else,' she said apologetically, dropping a bombshell.

'Must be some mistake.' Henry smiled, but his heart was beating just that little bit faster. 'I booked the rooms through the Internet and I have a confirmation e-mail.' He tapped his back pocket and kept his voice reasonable.

'I know, I'm sorry.' Henry saw her gulp. 'I assumed that because of the weather you wouldn't be coming.' She shrugged awkwardly, not really knowing what to do with her body language.

'I would have informed you if that had been the case.' His voice had become as cold as the weather.

'I'm sorry, but the rooms have been let to someone else now.'

'We'll have two more rooms, then.'

'I have only the two rooms, unfortunately.'

Moments before Henry had been half-visualizing this woman naked, a sad trait he'd had, since being a penis-led teenager, of mentally undressing women as soon as he met them, and one that